Books by Ella Thorp Ellis

Where the Road Ends
Roam the Wild Country
Riptide
Celebrate the Morning

Where the Road Ends

Where the Road Ends

ELLA THORP ELLIS

Atheneum 1974 New York

Copyright © 1974 by Ella Thorp Ellis
All rights reserved
Library of Congress catalog card number 73-84824
ISBN 0-689-30134-0
Published simultaneously in Canada by
McClelland & Stewart, Ltd.
Manufactured in the United States of America
by Halliday Lithograph Corporation
West Hanover, Massachusetts
First Edition

For Dave

Where the Road Ends

One

Above the deserted California beach ran an old highway that could not meet the demands of the evening rush, and so honking and braking blended with the pounding of the incoming tide. It was June, and summer tourists added to the normal traffic.

Pete heard this as he slumped on a driftwood log beneath the overhanging cliff. He heard the gulls, too. And the wind. He was aware that the wind dumped dirt and exhaust fumes on him before it raked across the strip of sand and pulled the sea into crosshatches of white foam, exposing the riptides. He would not want to swim this stretch, even if it weren't so cold, and even if he were not the only one on the beach. He tried to laugh at himself for feeling alone with the highway directly above but he could not, anymore than he could take off the pack on his back or stand up to gather firewood as he knew he must, and soon.

3

It would be dark in less than an hour. He absolutely must get up and scrounge driftwood for his fire. It wouldn't be easy because the beach appeared to be picked bare. Perhaps he should take out the peanut butter sandwiches he'd brought for lunch and eat them.

Instead he remained motionless, hugging his arms against his chest, much as he had since early afternoon, staring at the ocean. Why had he run away? Maybe because of the ocean? But there it was, coming and going, and all he could think was that a man could drown out there.

"Never mind, I'm *still* better off here on this beach. Better off without *them*. And it will be warm enough once I get to the Virgin Islands," he said aloud, his anger whipping the words.

He stood up, then, as if the words, spoken aloud, had released him. He shrugged off his pack, stowing it carefully in the purple ice plant that grew down the cliff, so it would be out of the sand. He should have found out whether rangers raked the beach with spotlights, kicking off sleepers.

"Just let them try and kick *me* out. I can outsleep *any* cop with *any* spotlight tonight," he shouted, waving a clenched fist. He stood a moment, his head cocked to one side, as if listening for an echo that did not come. Then he walked down to the tide line and watched the sandpipers darting through foam left by the tide, hunting for sand crabs, but wary of the surging water. They were running away too, he thought.

Half the sun had disappeared below the horizon before he set out to hunt for wood, but by the time the cars on the highway above had turned on their lights, like fireflies, he had a small fire. Enough wood for another hour or two, and a start for breakfast. His stew bubbled over the open flame, and the sight and the smell gave him a curious warm pride, as if he had grown the potatoes and carrots instead of scooping them out of the can.

"I'm going home. I'm on my way. They can't hardly stop me now," he said softly, watching the gray smoke from his fire curl against the darkening sky. Then he saw that his was the only fire on the beach and realized it might be illegal. He would have to put it out soon.

He did douse the fire after dinner and, because it grew cold, he crawled into his sleeping bag. Usually he liked to lie awake on the beach and watch for falling stars while he listened to the surf, but tonight he lay clenching his eyes closed, shivering although he was not cold.

No matter what happened he would not go back. If the beach patrol found him, they could take him but no one could make him stay. Not after what he overheard last night. He'd come home from the library and stood on the dark square of front lawn, curious as to why they were still at the kitchen table, his foster parents and their son, Johnny. He'd listened.

"Well, I don't care what you say. You won't listen to me so I can't stop you from adopting Pete, but just don't get the idea he'll ever be *my* brother, because I don't even like the guy and I never will."

"Son, I know. He's so sure of himself about every blessed thing in this world sometimes I want to shake the daylights out of him myself."

"He thinks he's Jesus Christ Almighty," Johnny added. Pete watched through the window and saw his foster father nod, his face tight and angry.

"I never once feel like I've gotten through to him—like he—tolerated me."

"But he needs us," his foster mother said quietly, in a pleading tone that had made Pete turn and run. The sickness of his needing and that wheedling tone made him run far into the night, reliving all other humiliations. In the morning, after they were out of the house, he'd packed and left a note, thanking them for taking care of him the last three years. He'd thought of saying more, but the memory of *her* voice and *his* face returned, and he signed his full name with a flourish. *Peter Anthony Logan.*

"*He* wanted to sock me in the jaw. That's what he really wanted," Pete muttered into the sleeping bag. All night he worried about a beach patrol, waking each time he heard a motor or the soft whoosh of tires sinking into the loose sand. He'd press his eyes more tightly shut against the expected flash of light. But no one bothered him.

The next morning as he lay watching dawn break over the ocean, the morning star was all that was left of the grim night. No one would hustle him now. By daylight the beach was his. He knew better than to lay claim to the ocean, but the gulls, diving for perch, were his friends.

Still, it had been an exhausting time, and Pete groaned and pulled the sleeping bag back over his head. There was no point in getting up so early.

He woke again when he felt someone standing over him, breathing down on him.

He froze. Slowly, slowly he turned on his side and peeked through the metal teeth of his partially unzipped sleeping bag. He stared at cowboy boots, unpolished, run over at the heel, and at least size thirteen. They were less than a foot from his face. Gradually, against his will, his eyes traveled up tight Levi's, blue-and-white plaid shirt, a dirty cowhide jacket, and stared into a big smiling face. Smiling, remember that, he thought as he closed his eyes, but with his eyes closed he couldn't be sure the face *had* been friendly.

He peeked again and saw that the intruder outweighed him by about twenty-five pounds and was a boy about his own age. About fifteen. Red hair. Freckles. His hair was curly and waved to his shoulder like Jesus Christ's. He had brown eyes, gentle eyes. In one hand he kept rolling a pair of dice and they clinked against his ring, over and over.

"You're awake," the stranger said. "I'm Barney O'Shaughnessy."

Pete nodded and propped himself on one elbow in his sleeping bag. It was warmer outside than he'd expected. He needed to go to the bathroom, but here was this guy.

"Hey, I am sorry—you are Pete Logan, aren't you?" the boy asked in a gravelly voice.

"Yes," Pete admitted in a whisper. The last thing in the world he needed was someone who knew who he was. He peered closely at the freckled face with the long red hair and vaguely remembered passing it in the dark halls at school. But they'd never been in a class together, he was sure of that. Pete waited. Summer vacation had just started so he should have expected other campers.

"I said I was sorry. I'm cold, and I don't have any matches. Mind if I start your fire?"

"Help yourself. Matches are in the pack," Pete mumbled, heading over the cold sand toward the portable rest rooms. It was only as he walked back to his camp, enjoying the slightly fishy smells of drying seaweed and wet sand, that he realized how stupid he'd been. He invited a complete stranger, a guy he'd only seen in the halls at school, to go through his pack. He felt the money belt around his waist. At least he had that. Two hundred dollars between him and starvation.

The boy, Barney, squatted before the orange flames, warming his hands. It was a good fire, and the smoke was already dissipating, so that only a thin gray ribbon of it drifted toward the sea. Not many guys could make that clean a fire.

Pete tried to figure the boy squatting before the fire, because it might be important to know whether he was apt to talk about their meeting. Pete wasn't going back. He was sure in his mind about that but it would make a difference if he could travel at his own pace or if he had to put a thousand miles between himself and California before he could draw breath. Hard to tell. This guy looked like the friendly type who was apt to keep talking.

"Thanks again," Barney said. "I was so mad last night I just grabbed my jacket and bolted. Along about two this morning—brrrr."

"Fight with your folks?" Pete asked eagerly. He dumped the last of his canteen water into a dehydrated omelet mixture and put the frying pan over a portable grill. "There's plenty for two," he added.

"Great. Actually, I guess the trouble is that I don't fight with my grandmother. She just says we're moving and that's it. I've never finished a year in the same school. We haul the trailer into a town, settle in, she harvests one crop of green onions and lettuce around the wheels and

8

we're off again. This year I had general math in Arkansas and then came out here and was supposed to know geometry. The year before it was algebra in three different parts of Florida—"

"You want to be a mathematician or something?"

"Ha! If I were old enough, I'd quit math *and* school. How about you?"

"I'm going to be a marine biologist," Pete said. He found the words reassuring; the one settled decision in his whole life.

Barney looked at him curiously but said nothing. Pete was tempted to tell him everything. After all, he'd run away too. But there was a look in Barney's face, the same look Johnny had had when he had tried to tell *him* about the ocean. A look that said Pete was putting on airs. And the terrible loneliness as they lay in the dark room night after night waiting for sleep and would not talk. Not that he blamed Johnny for not liking him. His parents had brought Pete into the house to be a good example and *then* made their son share his room, too. But Pete hadn't done anything to *Barney*. He was giving *him* breakfast. What did *Barney* care what he wanted to do? Still, probably Barney and Johnny would have talked all night. Not that it mattered.

"Could you get some water? Thought I'd make some cocoa," Pete said coldly.

"Sure thing. Sorry."

"Nothing to be *sorry about*," Pete muttered after the retreating cowboy boots.

"One thing, though, you're sure a great pole-vaulter. I bet you make varsity next year. Sure wish I'd be there to see you," Barney said a few minutes later and the face

Pete looked into was open and admiring. "You make it look easy—going over."

"Maybe," Pete shrugged. Giving up track had been the hardest part about leaving, and he'd rather not think about it. He worked quickly, finishing breakfast. He liked cooking, and he hummed a little while he split English muffins and set out plates. He only had one set of silver but Barney could use the fork and he'd take the spoon.

The cooking eggs, muffins, and cocoa took on a charcoal tang and blended with the salt air. Whenever Pete was cooking for himself, he always fixed breakfasts because they smelled good. Any time of day.

"Sure smells delicious," Barney said, rolling his dice in his left hand, waiting.

"Dig in, then." Pete made room for the cocoa pan over the best heat by dishing out the omelet and muffins. "You going on today, Barney?"

"What I been thinking—I could hide out here on the beach until she's gone and then maybe she'd let me stay— what I mean is, she trusts me, and if she knew how important—who am I kidding? I'll probably go on back to Florida with her. Nothing short of dying is ever going to stop Lily moving on. My old man was the same way— trucker—" Barney sighed and ate silently.

If we could only trade places, Barney boy, Pete thought. Florida was just a hop and a skip from the blue Caribbean, and the Virgin Islands where Pete was heading. Again he was tempted to tell Barney, and again he decided against it. Anyone so free and easy with his own business would share Pete's, too.

"Say, you practice vaulting much over the summer?" Barney asked.

Two

Before nine they were ready to go. The dishes were washed and packed, the fire doused with water and then covered with sand, and the garbage lay in the trash can waiting for marauding sea gulls.

"You heading toward town—maybe we could hike on back together?" Barney suggested, standing on the other side of a wet spot in the sand that had been their fire.

Pete heard the eagerness in the question, and he hesitated. He listened to the dice hitting Barney's ring and then to the surf and finally admitted the sound of the traffic picking up on the highway above. Near them a flock of gulls rose in a dark cloud and headed out to sea, probably sensing a school of perch. It was only June so they should still be close in. In his mind he saw the silver fish somersault out of the water into the sunlight, again and again. But Barney shifted his feet uneasily and, with a wrench, Pete came back to the decision he must make.

"How soon's your grandmother leaving?" he asked tentatively.

"Guess I didn't ask. But Lily isn't one to sit around making lists. She moves. Why?" Barney continued scuffing the sand.

Pete nodded, adjusted the pack on his back, and stuck out his hand. "Well—I guess this is sayonara then. I'm heading down the coast a way." It would have been good to have company, but he wouldn't want to be blamed if Barney missed his grandmother and got left behind. He would not want that responsibility.

"Oh—well—thanks for the breakfast. I was really hungry," Barney said, as if hunger were new and strange to him. "I hope we'll run into each other before I leave. Say, how far are you going?"

"Depends. I'll go on until I feel like staying." Pete was pleased by the admiration on Barney's face. Again he was tempted to tell him about running away and heading toward the Virgin Islands and an aunt he'd never met. He'd like to hear it said out loud, hear how it sounded, to put that final seal on his future. He shifted his pack, about to take it off, when he remembered how easily Barney talked. He hesitated.

"That's the kind of parents to have—Lily wants to know where I'll be—every hour."

"Why do you call her Lily if she's your grandmother?"

Barney shrugged. "I don't know. Always have. My dad did too."

"I'm an orphan." Pete was horrified at what he'd admitted.

"Say, so am I. At least my dad died—driving a semi-trailer in a snowstorm—went over an embankment—I was eleven."

"That's hard," Pete said, wanting to turn and run. His own parents had been killed in an automobile accident. He'd been four and he hardly remembered them, but he could tell that Barney could see that truck going over the icy shoulder and it was a big thing in his life. Pete didn't want to stay talking any longer with a guy who remembered his father so well. He'd always hated it when boys at school boasted about their fathers. It made him uncomfortable in some way he couldn't quite pin down. Besides, this guy already knew too much about *him*. "Look, I've really got to get going. I'll see you around."

Pete shook hands and started quickly up the gravel trail that wound from the beach to the highway above. He heard Barney call his name but only waved without turning or slowing. There was no point in trading addresses, since neither of them would be having one for a while. And they could stand about on one foot and another all morning at the rate they were going. It was better to make a clean break. He pulled at his pack and kicked at the gravel. It wasn't as if he weren't used to going it alone, after all, and Barney probably wouldn't like him so well if they got better acquainted.

He felt a weariness, possibly only because the trail led in a steep arc up the cliff instead of making the switchbacks more usual to that grade. The loose pebbles made it tricky to keep his footing, and Pete only briefly noted the beach lupine and the poppies that fanned out on either side of the trail. It was nerve-racking to hear Barney bounding along as if he knew the way in his sleep, making Pete feel like a tenderfoot. He stepped up his own pace.

Nevertheless, about halfway up the trail Barney caught up. Pete stepped aside to let him pass. He was pleased that the redhead was also puffing and that his face was already flushed.

"Hey, Pete, I forgot—"

"Go on ahead, speedy. We can talk at the top."

Barney gave him a peculiar look, shrugged, skirted him, and drove on. He had a curious lope, as if, like a jackrabbit, he gathered the strength for each leap in his forelimbs. But then, instead of landing on his hands, he would paw at the air while his legs made the actual advance.

Suddenly, something went wrong. Barney's feet began to slide, sending rumbling gravel down the path. Barney came backward like someone out of a slapstick movie, hands stretched out, body stiff; Pete watched him coming and snickered. It had to be a joke. Only when the first pebbles hit *his* shin did he fully understand that Barney was falling.

"Grab a bush, Barney! Hey, stop!" Pete's throat felt dry and he grabbed a lupine bush himself as Barney slid past him and rolled off to one side, landing just off the path. He saw Barney crumple and stop and groan and, as he started toward him, Pete lost his own footing. His hands groped, catching just an instant on the dewy lupine leaves. and then he heard the crack as the branch broke off and he started to slide himself, ever so slowly, damp leaves still clutched in one hand. The gravel hurt through his tennis shoes as he tried to dig in his heels. He reached over to grab another bush. There seemed plenty of time but he slid past that bush and then, still reaching, slow motion, his pack pitched him head over heels down the loose gravel.

"Damn you!" His voice seemed to follow him down a

hundred feet. He hit on the sharp angle of the pots through his pack, and he worried that they'd be wrecked or the pack torn. He smelled sagebrush but could not find it to break his fall. He heard rocks and Barney's voice and cars honking, but through the dust he could see almost nothing, could only wait until he bumped on his pack and somersaulted again.

If he didn't close his eyes, he might still grab—something. But his bloody clutching hands caught nothing, and he cursed them impersonally, as if they were no longer attached to him.

His pack should be helping, but it only tilted him, so that he bumped harder on his right side. Then he tried twisting to slow down, wrenching his body painfully; but still he picked up momentum.

And then it was over. He hit a boulder, bounced, and struck a bush. The avalanche he started went on down the path, sliding slowly into the sand. Then there was a moment of complete and utter silence. And out of the silence he heard his own scream. For a moment he did not know why he screamed; he had time to be ashamed even, before the waves of pain came in colored succession. A pain so terrible he knew two things: something was broken and he was alive.

"Smashed it good," he heard himself whisper. "Like old Humpty-Dumpty." And he knew in the pain that he couldn't be put back together either. He'd remain splayed over that bush forever.

"Lie still. I'll phone your parents. Can you say your number—never mind, I'll find—Pete, I'm sorry—"

Pete heard himself, "Damn you, now you've *done* it— doctor—don't leave me!"

15

Sometime later he found himself covered with Barney's jacket.

"Doctor?" he asked.

"I'm going now. I was afraid to leave you, passed out like that. Where does it hurt?"

Pete saw that Barney was crying. As if I'm already dead, he thought. "Don't leave me—please!" He was sick with shame at the whimper in his voice, the begging.

"But you've *got* to have a doctor. Can you walk? Maybe we could get a ride if we could make it to the highway—" Barney sounded doubtful.

Pete nodded. He didn't know if his legs worked, but he'd need Barney's help to find out. And it would keep Barney with him, in case he passed out again. He was afraid to be alone with the pain, on this cliff where he might yet tumble all the way to the bottom, rolling as he'd heard the gravel roll on by him until its scratch disappeared into the yellow sand. Suddenly Pete remembered something and clutched for his money belt, slumping in relief that it was still there. He nodded to Barney. He was ready to try and stand.

"First, we'll have to get you out of that pack." The perspiration stood out on Barney's forehead and Pete watched it mix with the drying tears as the bigger boy tried to slip Pete's pack over his shoulders. Pain tore through him, leaving him shaking uncontrollably. Pete shook his head—one shoulder wouldn't work.

"Then we'll have to cut the straps," Barney said.

"No—whatever—leave those straps! Here, try again!"

"The right arm?" Barney was gentle and also surprisingly efficient. The pain would pass, nothing to Pete beside the terrible threat of cutting the straps. He'd worked

16

six months for this backpack, and without it he couldn't travel. He'd be through. He gritted his teeth and made no sound while they slipped it off,

"There," Barney sighed.

It was an effort for Pete to see clearly. He focused on Barney's boots. He saw also his dream of the Virgin Islands fading like some pain-induced mirage—unless he could stand. "I won't go back," he said aloud.

"Here, lean your left side, the good side, on me and we'll see if you can stand," Barney said.

"The pack?"

"I'll come back for it."

Three

When he found that his legs still functioned, Pete knew he had a chance. It was about a hundred feet to the top of the cliff. The cliff was craggy and rocky and it would be easy to slip again. Winter storms had eaten away at the soft rock and patches of ice plant and lupine grew sporadically and he might slide on them. Already the sun beat down and a haze hung over the ocean. There was no breeze. It was going to be a miserable climb, but for Pete there was no alternative. He thought he might die if he were left alone.

A wave of nausea twisted his stomach and he felt drawn out into the roar of the breakers, the pounding starting in his stomach and echoing inside his aching head.

"I'm ready," he said.

First Barney let him lean against his side but that was too painful and Pete found that having support from

18

the back worked better. As Barney pushed and they gradually began to inch their way up the cliff, Pete felt as if he were in a dream, his own recurring dream of fighting through dense clumps of seaweed while the riptide kept pulling him farther and farther from shore. Only when they reached the highway would he be safe. Never mind the pain, he had to make each step.

He kept looking up toward the highway, trying to focus on the hum of the traffic and the smell of exhausts. He ached all over but the pain in his right shoulder and arm was terrible, and he suddenly remembered a blue jay he'd seen once whose wing trailed uselessly on the ground. The bird kept pecking and pecking at the wing. Struggling up the trail, he understood that bird.

Finally, somehow, they made it up to the highway. Pete felt his legs giving way and sank to the drying grass by the side of the road, propping himself against a boulder while Barney went back for the pack. He'd made it.

When Barney came back, he placed the pack so that it made a backrest, better than the boulder. Pete wondered foggily where Barney had learned such a gentle touch. There was no shade, and the exhausts and the smell of the macadam highway were nauseating. Pete watched helplessly as Barney tried to get a ride. Not many cars came by this late in the morning and those that did would slow and then, when they caught sight of Pete, speed up and round the corner out of sight.

"Too bad you didn't bleed more, Pete. Then someone might stop. Maybe I should hike out to the nearest phone —what do you think?"

"There's no one to phone."

"You must live with *someone*," Barney said, squatting beside him. He said nothing more but took out his dice and started rolling them in his left hand.

"Stop that! You could drive a guy crazy with those, you know that? I was in a foster home but something happened—I'd rather not talk about it—and I left yesterday—and I'll never go back, never." Pete thought he might pass out again and he concentrated on shallow breathing, which he'd heard helped.

"That's all right. None of my business. But where will you go, what'll you *do?*"

"I have an aunt in the Virgin Islands, and I was heading there." Pete frowned. "I mean, I *am* heading there."

"Then you won't be back at the high school next fall either, and you would have made the varsity track team sure." There was awe in Barney's voice.

It mattered.

"Doesn't matter." He'd worked two years to make that team, but he couldn't go back and there was no use thinking about it.

Pete felt guilty because he'd let on he was going to see this aunt, and it wasn't true. He might go by and see her but he'd be on his own and he was going *there* because that was one of the best places to study fish. But Barney wouldn't understand that. Nobody did. Besides, Barney couldn't really be an orphan if he had a grandmother, could he? Pete felt too tired to figure it out. If only he could get to some shade. Or get away from the smell of exhausts. But it was hopeless, endless. And suppose they did finally get a ride? He didn't even know the name of *any* doctor. Probably the best thing would be to drop off at a hospital and ask. He had the money to pay, money he'd earned picking apples last summer and fortunately kept in his own account. What was Barney holding up for him to see—a sign of some sort, but the lettering was too faint to read.

"Hey, what's it say?"

Barney turned the sign toward him again. It was only pencil on cardboard, but finally Pete made out the letters H-E-L-P. He nodded and tried to smile but the nodding sent pain through his shoulder and on out to the tips of his fingers, which also felt numb, like they were asleep. He winced.

"Only two cars have come by since I got it made," Barney called from the edge of the highway where he stood.

"I think there's a black felt pen in my pack—the outside pocket." Pete wondered at the numbness in his fingers. He would have tried to shake them awake if his arm was working.

The felt pen must have done the trick because the very next car, an old white Dodge, pulled over and stopped just beyond them.

An older man, maybe thirty, wearing Levi's and a purple satin shirt, came running back. He was laughing.

"Well, first time I've ever seen *that* sign. What's the trouble?"

"My friend here hurt his arm, took a spill," Barney told the man.

"I think it's broken. My shoulder won't work either," Pete added, ashamed of the pleading in his voice.

"Well, hop in and we'll see what we can do." The man swung Pete's pack on his back and Pete worried that maybe he wouldn't wait for them, would simply take off with his pack. He signaled Barney to keep up with the man in the purple shirt.

"Relax. He's OK. Let me help you up. You'd think that pack was your life, the way you hang on to it."

"It is. Go ahead. I'd rather make it on my own." And only when he saw Barney sitting in the white Dodge did Pete start his own painful trek to the car. He climbed in the back and lay against the cushions, giving in to the pain and fatigue. He was drenched in sweat.

"Thank God, that's over," Barney muttered as he closed the door.

"Where to?"

"Central Hospital," Pete said.

"Haversford Trailer Court, Fourth and Mason Streets. My grandmother will take us to *our* doctor," Pete heard Barney say.

"No—don't tell your grandmother."

"She's OK. You'll see. And I won't say anything I don't have to, relax. Please, sir, Haversford Trailer Court. It's this side of Sebastopol."

"No." But Pete didn't really care. He'd walk away if they let him off at the trailer court. He'd gotten one ride. He could get another. At least he was out of the sun. And that was worth a lot.

The first thing Pete saw when they pulled into the bush-lined driveway of the trailer court was a barefoot woman watering her garden. She held the hose almost straight up, spraying great arcs of water over one of the smallest vegetable gardens he'd ever seen, half a dozen heads of lettuce and some green onions.

"Lily says you have to spray high so the water can

collect energy from the air and give it to the plants," Barney explained.

"What *else* does she say?" their driver asked.

Pete stared. The next thing he knew Barney hopped out of the car and threw his arms around the woman, spraying them both and also wetting down Pete's pack, which Barney held.

"Turn off that water!" shouted Pete, climbing stiffly out of the car.

After the water was finally turned off, Barney introduced his grandmother. She must have been in her fifties, a pretty woman with very pink cheeks and laughing brown eyes. But it was the yellow satin bows tying off her gray ponytails and the short, green silk jump suit and the floppy lime-colored garden hat that set her apart from other grandmothers Pete had met. That and the fact that she did not seem in the least surprised to see her runaway grandson or Pete or the man who brought them.

"Hey, Barney, leave it here," Pete said as the redhead took his pack and stowed it inside a large trailer. Barney didn't answer, and he felt too weak to protest further.

"Well, I thank you, Mister. You not only returned my Barney, here, but brought along a bonus. Where did you collect them?" Lily added in an offhand way that made Pete watch her closely.

"Interstate 101 above the beach. They had a big HELP sign. I'm afraid I've brought you damaged goods, Ma'am. Sure you can manage? I'm due at work, but I could call my boss."

"We'll manage fine, and we thank you, we sure do. Nothing here that can't be mended, I imagine. Barney, get your friend in on the bed. Looks like he's about to pass out on us. Thanks again," she called over the running motor of the old Dodge.

"All right then, what happened to *you*, young man? Looks to me like you may be wanting a doctor before the day is out." She came striding into the trailer and put a hand on Pete's forehead.

"I won't go back," Pete moaned, shaking his head as he lay down on a bed that smelled of lavender. He closed his eyes.

"Considering your condition, I don't think I'd want to either. ·Your right side?"

"It's his arm and shoulder, Lily. We were on a trail, and he tried to stop my fall and he fell. No, I'm fine and —I'm sorry about last night." Barney's voice dropped.

"You *called* her Lily," Pete whispered.

"That's right. I stand in the relation of grandmother to Barney, but as a human being I answer to Lily. Remember that, Pete."

It was comforting to hear her use his name. She seemed all right and she didn't ask many questions and she had that good smile, but it wasn't until later, when they pulled up in front of the three-story medical building barricaded with venetian blinds, that Pete breathed easy. Then he knew they weren't headed for Juvenile Hall.

"You have any money with you?" Lily asked.

Pete nodded. "I'll be fine now. It's nothing. Really. Thanks for the lift—and everything," he said firmly. "I won't take anymore of your time."

Four

Lily jumped out of the pickup truck and came around to Pete's side. Then there was a moment when the boy and the woman both had hold of the door handle, pulling it at opposites. Pete gave way, and the door opened, revealing the long step down to the green lawn strip that separated him from the less precarious footing of the sidewalk. Lily put out her arm, and he was forced to lean on her, making him feel ungrateful when he said a little harshly,

"You've both been great but I can handle myself from here. I know you've got lots to do. Sayonara, Barney."

"How about your pack?" Barney asked quietly.

They stared at each other. It was noon, and people pushed and hurried along the sidewalk on their way to lunch, to squeeze in errands, to meet a friend. It was a free time, and everyone hurried to use it. Over this crowd the boys assessed each other. Pete knew there must be some way to cope with his pack if he could only think clearly, but he could not possibly carry it. He also knew that Barney realized he'd *have* to help just when Pete wanted him out of the picture.

"I'm sorry. It has nothing to do with you, Barney. It's just that I've *got* to get out of this town."

"But we're not *stopping* you, only trying to help."

"Not yet," Pete muttered, looking across to where Lily stood holding open one of the heavy glass doors, waiting for him. "Don't you *realize* your grandmother may feel it's her duty to turn me in—any minute?"

Barney shook his head. "Let's go," he said gently. "You were the one who insisted on bringing this pack."

It occurred to Pete that he might have to leave the pack in order to get free of them and out of town on his own. He considered how long he might have to work to buy another. He sighed and started toward Lily and the open door.

"Is a general practitioner all right with you?" Lily asked. "They generally charge less." She flipped through the doors and had finished dialing by the time he reached the row of telephone booths. "You can't just walk in and see any doctor, you know. They want appointments and, besides, just your luck to get one who only delivers babies."

"No," Pete said, not knowing exactly what he was denying.

Lily paid no attention. "Yes, there was an accident. A fall. Damage to the arm and shoulder. Of course, we understand that. We'll be right up." She hung up and turned to them, smiling.

"No!"

26

"Third floor. Room 309," Lily said. "Let's catch that elevator."

"Didn't I tell you it was hard to fight with her?" Barney added as the elevator door closed behind them.

Pete did not answer. He had to let them *do* something, and then maybe they'd go. Meanwhile, he waited, suspended between floors in the dull cranking elevator and later in a crowded waiting room, sustained by the reassuring whiff of disinfectant each time the door to the doctor's office swung open. He was in pain and his effort to rid himself of Lily had taken his last energy, but he rested like Brer Fox, with one eye open, while Lily arranged things with nurses and Barney kept talking about the time he broke his leg. He even heard himself answer, out of some depth of fatigue, and his polite toneless voice was that of a stranger. Which was not surprising, since he should be on the beach at Santa Cruz and his presence in this waiting room was totally due to this redheaded stranger and his grandmother who dressed like a leafing tree.

Pete laughed softly, in spite of himself, as he looked at Lily and realized the contrast between her and the other people in the room. Just like him to be taken in by a freak.

"What's so funny?" Barney asked, looking up from a sports article.

Pete smiled and shook his head. "What took you so long?" he asked as Lily came back from the nurse's desk.

"Case history. They'll have to fit us in."

"Hey, *what* did you tell her?" Pete tried to keep his voice casual.

"Don't say 'hey' to me, young man."

"I'm sorry but—"

"What I told them is innocuous. They're satisfied, but I'm not. Let's start with where you *are* headed." Lily kept her voice low.

"The Virgin Islands," Barney put in.

Pete looked up and saw that everyone in the waiting room was staring at them. They were the focus of attention. "You have the *biggest* mouth," he whispered fiercely.

"Yes, you keep out of this, Barney O'Shaughnessy. Why the Virgin Islands?" Lily glanced around the room and everyone dropped their eyes and took up their magazines again. "Busybodies."

"I have an aunt there," Pete answered uncomfortably. Going to study fish was obviously not going to make it with this lady.

"You're not inventing her?"

"No." And, as it happened, he was not. Aunt Lenore *did* exist. She was his father's sister. She did live in the Virgin Islands, and a book she had sent one Christmas *had* given him the marine biology bug. That was the best present she had ever sent; usually there were just shirts or a couple of dollars in the picture card. Every year she sent this card with a photograph of the family standing on a beach, and it was always this man with his arm around a woman and a girl, with palm trees in the background. The man got balder each year, and the little girl kept getting taller and better looking; but his aunt always looked about the same, and he could never remember from year to year what that was. He tried because he figured she must look like his father, whom he also couldn't remember, but it didn't work. Still, it had always comforted him that he did have a real family, like other people.

28

However, he wasn't going to camp with them. He'd introduce himself, but what happened then depended on them, on whether they liked *him*. But if it satisfied Lily, fine.

She said nothing further for several minutes. She appeared to be in deep thought and kept drawing in on her mouth as if she were making points to herself. Pete watched her as he flipped uneasily through an old magazine he'd seen before, waiting for her to suggest phoning the Virgin Islands, or something equally bad. He noticed Barney kept glancing at his grandmother, too.

"She *does* know you're coming?" Lily asked finally.

"She invited me!" Year before last she had said she hoped she'd be able to meet him someday.

"And you haven't done anything—so you're in trouble with the law?"

"No, my problem seems to be that I'm too goody-goody." Pete couldn't hide the bitterness.

Lily laughed. "Nothing more wearing."

"Peter Logan. The doctor will see you now."

Pete scrambled up, dropping his magazine in his hurry. He stood looking down, and he knew that he'd pass out if he tried to bend to the floor and pick it up. If he did *not,* Lily would feel she had to stick around and take care of him. He could feel the sweat trickling down his face.

"Here, I'll get it," Barney said, scooping up the magazine and slapping it back on the pile. "Good luck."

"One moment," Lily said.

No matter what, she was *not* coming into the examining room with him.

"They're waiting for me."

Lily held up one finger. "You said you have enough money to handle this. Might take twenty-five dollars."

Pete nodded. "I've got it."

"Then I'll be running along. I've got to get my laundry done."

Pete grinned. This was going to be easier than he'd expected.

"Oh, I'll be back before you're through, young man. Barney, you just hang around here in case he needs some help. The doctor will probably want X rays, and that always takes an hour or so. Should give me time." She frowned at her watch.

"That's what you think," Pete muttered as he went into the doctor's office. He would be long gone before she came back.

As it turned out, Barney's grandmother was right about the X rays. The doctor felt the shoulder, the arm, wrote a few lines, and the next thing Pete knew he was being wheeled down the hall in a wheelchair. He'd had a shot to ease the pain and kept falling asleep. They had to wake him when it was time for the X rays and again when the doctor was ready to read them.

"You're a lucky young man," the doctor said, holding the transparency up to the light. "I thought there might be a break in the shoulder but apparently you've just dislocated it and pulled some tendons. It's going to be very painful for a few days and maybe considerably longer while those tendons heal. I want you to wear a sling as long as the pain gives you any trouble and check back with me if you have any trouble with numbness or any paralysis—can't tell if a nerve might be damaged."

Pete peered at the transparency of his arm and shoul-

30

der while the doctor continued to feel along his shoulder. "First X ray I ever saw. It's weird. I mean, like I've already died and my bones are picked clean."

"That's a good way to put it. You feel like you're getting a look into your future. I'm going to try and pop that shoulder back into place. May hurt a bit—there we go—steady—easy now. *There,* that's all there is to it." The doctor looked pleased with himself.

It felt as if he were breaking the shoulder to Pete, but in only a minute or so, while he was still on the examining table, the shoulder felt as if it worked. It worked! He'd be able to use it! He could go on to the Virgin Islands. "Oh, thanks, thanks a lot," he said, and the pain and the dizziness didn't matter. He could sleep for a day or so, and he'd be fine.

"All right, that should do it," the doctor said, slipping a white cotton sling around his shoulder and tying it behind his neck. "Suppose you come back in a couple of weeks, and we'll see how it looks," he added, helping Pete into his shirt and off the table.

Pete nodded. He should be in Texas in two weeks, maybe even as far as Florida. "You just don't know how great it is that you could fix it—my shoulder—thanks," he added awkwardly.

He left the comforting smell of the disinfectant and went back to the waiting room reluctantly. If there had been a back way, he would have taken it and avoided Barney completely. He knew where he was going. To the bus station and out of this town quickly and forever, as far as Santa Cruz and a motel where he could rest the arm for a day and then look around for a job. Or maybe he'd take the nearly two hundred bucks he'd have left after paying the doctor bill and get a plane ticket and go clear across country with it. He could work when he got to Florida. If he could only lie down on a soft bed and sleep and get away from the pain for about twelve hours, he'd know which was best to do.

He heard that strange high voice of hers first and then saw the old lady sitting cross-legged, still in those funny green silk pants, smoking a cigarette, waving it in jerking arcs as if she were still watering, as she explained something to Barney. She wore yellow tennis shoes now, and she kept circling one foot. Without exception every single person in the waiting room was watching her. Even the babies. He sighed. Poor Barney.

"But can I go, too?" Barney was asking as he came in.

"Don't see why not. You have to get over to Florida, and if one way is more fun than another, take it! Hi, Pete, what did the sawbones say?"

"Says I just dislocated my shoulder and pulled a few tendons. So it's nothing. Barney, let go of my pack."

"Was he able to pop it back in?" Lily asked.

"How would you like a ride as far as Texas?" Barney asked.

Pete looked from one to the other. They both looked like the cat that swallowed the canary, they were so excited. But they were out of their minds if they thought he could wait around until grandma pulled out her lettuce and got ready to leave. This town was dangerous for him.

"Yes, the shoulder's back in," Pete answered, wondering if he could possibly carry his pack. Knowing he could not.

"Could you leave today, in about an hour?" Lily asked.

"That's about what I'd been planning."

"Lily says I can come with you."

Pete stared. Was there no end to the nerve of these two? First this guy tumbled him down a hillside—

"Lily says there's this guy at the trailer court on his way to Texas, and he'll give us a ride. She says I have to go to Florida anyhow, and I might as well go the way I want." As Barney looked at Pete, his smile faded.

"He owns a couple of pitch games, and he's on his way to Texas to join up with his carnival. It won't be the most comfortable trip in the world because the shock absorbers in Carl's pickup are shot. But it won't cost you a red penny. Carl's worried about falling asleep at the wheel—had an accident once—so you just pay for your food and maybe a motel if we can't sleep out some night. Says he prefers to just throw a sleeping bag down by the road if he can, though. Nice guy. He's lived in our trailer court all winter."

"All the way to Texas without it costing," Pete said aloud. "You'd be going, but not your grandmother?"

"Oh, I've got odds and ends to clear up here, for both me and Barney, but I knew Carl had been hunting for a rider, and he says you're both welcome. Of course, you're on your own once you reach Texas."

Pete brightened. That was good news. This was really too good to turn down, especially now with the dislocation and all. Still—"All right, I'll *do* it," he said.

"But you don't want to?" Barney asked quietly.

"Oh, sure. Thanks, thanks a lot. It was just such a surprise is all." Pete couldn't understand why Barney should care. He could ride with the carnival man anyhow, couldn't he?

33

Lily stubbed out her cigarette. She stood up, her yellow tennis shoes hitting the tile floor with a smart slap so that the two or three people in the waiting room who had given up watching them jerked back to attention.

"Then it's settled. Let's move. We got to get Barney here fitted out. Barney, you take Pete's pack."

"Like you said, your grandmother really moves." Pete grinned at Barney as they left the waiting room, the two boys way behind Lily as she charged down the hall and out into the hot sun.

Five

Late that afternoon the boys and their driver, a man in his mid-thirties whose face was nearly hidden by a thick curling black beard, were heading south in a battered white pickup truck. They left the ripening orchards and wound through pasture and truck-farming country that clustered in homes as they drew closer to the San Francisco Bay area. The sun was still high, and it would have been easy to go on into San Jose that night but the driver knew of a spring that came out of a meadow scattered with oak trees, and he'd decided to camp there. He said he wanted to see if poppies were still blooming in the middle of June.

That had been almost all he had said in the hour or more they'd been on the road. They were all quiet, the three in the cab of the truck, as if surprised to find themselves in each other's company. Or perhaps it was only that after the noise and confusion with which Lily threw together Barney's gear, they were relieved to be on their way and let themselves be lulled by the rhythmic purr of motor and wheels and the sucking wind of a busy highway. The afternoon was also comfortably warm.

The driver cleared his throat, and Pete hoped he would not speak. A moment passed and he did not, and Pete sighed. He needed the silence. He would certainly have preferred to spend the night by himself in that motel room he'd dreamed of renting. Too much was happening too fast and he'd lost control somehow. He *was* grateful. This free ride would save him close to a hundred dollars, especially since he couldn't have worked the next few days anyhow because of the bad shoulder. Still. Still, he wouldn't have dislocated the shoulder if he hadn't invited Barney to breakfast—was it only this morning?— and that alone would have saved him the twenty-five dollars he'd paid in X ray and doctor's bills.

Pete tried to lean away from Barney but with three in the cab there was little room. The painkillers were wearing off, and the ache in his shoulder and arm was getting worse. The arm was swollen, and each time he bumped against the door he got an extra shock of pain.

Barney shouldn't even be there. What kind of a grandmother would say, "Fine. Meet me in Florida next month?" His foster parents would never have let *their* son make this kind of a trip. They wouldn't even have let *Pete* make the trip, and that thought gave him pleasure, since it proved his present freedom. But then he saw himself on that lawn looking in while they discussed him, and he shut his eyes and shook his head. Johnny must be glad to have his room back.

The driver swung onto the freeway exit, and Pete hit

the door jamb with his bad side. This time the pain waves enveloped him, and he was afraid he might vomit. If he said something the man would stop but Pete was supposed to keep him from falling asleep, not hold him up, and it wasn't a good idea to start right in being a nuisance. They'd stop soon, and then the pain would stop. It didn't mean anything, just curves and a bumpy exit road and bad shock absorbers. Soon they'd eat and fall asleep under a sky full of stars. Hang on, just hang on, he commanded himself, but the pain did not subside.

"You all right?" Barney asked. "I thought you were asleep."

"I was," Pete muttered.

"We'll be there pretty quick now, five more minutes," the man said. He had a gentle smile.

"I'm fine," Pete insisted, and he was surprised at how loud his voice sounded in the cab of the truck. It struck him that the driver looked like Paul Bunyan.

"Didn't they give you pain pills?" the man asked.

"Sure, and it must be time for another, Pete? Three hours."

Pete had been thinking it *must* be time, but he hated the open compassion on Barney's face. "I'll take one when I need it," he said, careful to keep his voice low and even.

"Oh, trying for brownie points, are you?" The driver sounded exasperated. "We don't give them around here, do we, Barney?" He raised one eyebrow, a habit he apparently had. Pete had watched him do this several times during the afternoon.

Barney shrugged, started to speak, then flushed and was quiet.

Pete drew the plastic vial out of his jacket pocket and

gulped a pain capsule. He was relieved when it slid smoothly because sometimes he gagged without water, and he would have died rather than fail before the driver.

The man nodded and smiled.

Pete pretended not to notice. He saw the eyebrow go up again. The man *was* a sarcastic slob but, on the whole, that might be easier to take than Barney's bleeding heart. At least you knew where you stood. The only real problem was that he did not know anything *about* this man except that he worried about falling asleep on the road and was headed for a carnival in El Paso. Not even his name. Lily had said his name, but Pete could only remember her standing in the trailer, flicking her cigarette into an empty milk bottle and telling Barney he needed four pairs of socks. Nothing of the man's name would be pulled back into that memory. Maybe he'd missed the name, worrying because *he* hadn't brought four pairs of socks, had only two and the one he was wearing.

The truck swung off the paved road onto a dirt spur that led up a gentle hill, through drying pasture colored with mustard and the poppies that were, indeed, still blooming. There was still an hour or so before sunset. The late afternoon sun hung over the rolling hills, slanting long shadows from big old oaks and, as it left a part of the meadow, closing poppies and buttercups in its wake. Small birds chattered as they hunted food and, overhead, a chicken hawk caught the downdrafts. Pete could see the hawk's shadow moving like a kite alongside their truck.

The man started to whistle as he pulled the truck up over the crest and down into a little valley, cupped and warmed by the surrounding hills. He drew to a stop beside an enormous oak and, still whistling, hopped out of the truck. He stretched, and then he knelt by a small barbecue pit someone had made of the rock outcroppings, peering into the ashes. A neat stack of wood lay next to the pit.

"Looks like we was expected." Barney laughed.

"Like I expected to return, you mean. I left this wood two–three months ago and it looks to me like no one's been by since. I worry about poachers some."

"Oh, you own this land?" Barney asked.

"No, but I love it, and that gives me *some* rights."

Pete listened, but Barney did not call the driver by name, although since they'd lived in the same trailer court all winter he *must* have learned it somewhere along the line. They appeared to know each other fairly well.

"Over here, Pete. We'll prop you right over here where you can lean back against this oak and tend our fire. That's your job, seeing our fire don't go out on us. Barney, you scrounge wood, and I'll see to the water," the man called back over his shoulder as he rolled out two sleeping bags against a huge oak tree.

Pete watched the two disappear into different parts of the woods, and then he stumbled over to the sleeping bags and collapsed. He was horrified to find he was crying. He pulled the extra bag over himself and lay there shivering, crying until gradually he was calmed, emptied out, exhausted even of pain. First, it occurred to him that he might have died if he'd been left alone with the bad arm and shoulder on that desolate wind-stripped beach. Later, he knew it was good fortune that he had this ride clear to Texas. Perhaps he could even get work at that carnival. It was something to think about. He would take off his sling by then. Maybe he and Barney could both get work. He hoped Barney understood that he hadn't been trying to get rid of him personally this morning. It was just that he had to get out of town. Pete fell asleep wondering what had happened to Barney's mother.

He woke to the smells of corned-beef hash and eggs frying in butter and the tantalizing aroma of coffee. The fire glowed, throwing little flames spurting out under the pans on the grill. He heard an owl and only then admitted what came with the good smells. It was dark, and he'd fallen asleep instead of tending fire.

"How do you feel?" Barney asked, handing him half a cantaloupe.

"Terrible—I was supposed to tend the fire. I'm sorry. Maybe I can do the dishes?"

"We would have routed you out except we didn't even have enough work for the two of us to do——" the man said.

"And guess who's been doing it *all?*"

"Tell your friend here why, Barney. Who wouldn't let the bet drop, who was so determined to have my hide with his dice? And don't let those eggs burn, boy."

"Sunny-side up, or over, Carl?" Barney asked, the edge on his voice controlled.

"Sunny-side will do nicely. The fact is, your buddy here took me for a sucker, bet me the whole evening's chores I couldn't roll two snake eyes out of six tries. Right?" The man rocked on his haunches lightly and then flipped his cigarette into the fire. The butt landed between the pots, and Barney jumped.

40

"Watch that butt. I wasn't taking you for a sucker. Didn't I tell you the odds are two hundred-to-one? Didn't I?" Barney said, handing Pete a plate on which both eggs had been broken and flipped.

Pete winked, and Barney shrugged. So his name was Carl, Pete thought, rubbing his eyes and pushing himself to a sitting position against the oak tree. He watched Barney break two more eggs carefully into the frying pan and then, surreptitiously, Pete took another pain pill. Barney had lost a bet and so he was doing the chores. So why was the driver rubbing it in?

Maybe he was just that kind of guy, this Carl? But Barney had said he was a good head and had wanted to make the trip. Pete looked at the dark man sitting on his heels, silhouetted against the fire. He was enjoying himself, either because the poppies were still blooming and his camp site waiting, or because he had someone to bait. His blue eyes rested on Barney, and he was smiling slightly. His dark hair was curly, even his neatly trimmed beard. A really good beard. He wore Levi's and a plaid shirt, but even in the firelight Pete could tell that the shirt was a Pendleton and the boots were expensive, maybe even made for him. He was tall and thin and carried himself like an athlete. How could he look like such a right person, when every time he opened his mouth he put someone down? Pete had long ago learned to be careful around put-down artists.

The man turned toward him. "Cat got your tongue?" he asked.

"Still waking up. How come you took the bet if you knew the odds?"

"Odds are for marks; so is betting for that matter.

But carnivals would close down and I'd have to cook if guys like Barney didn't think otherwise. Good eggs. Salt handy?"

"What's a mark?" Pete asked.

"Customer at a carnival, a gullible main source of money for the carny."

Barney handed him the salt, grinning now. "I'll get you tomorrow."

"See?" Carl laughed.

"Tea and coffee coming up," Barney called out from the fire, his voice disembodied by a sudden gust of smoke.

"I like that sunny-side up, too."

"And mixed, I reckon, Carl." Barney brought two pots and set them down on a flat rock. He flopped down himelf on the grass next to them. "Now be quiet, you all, while I wish on the evening star."

"God knows, I can tell you're a guy who'd better take help wherever it's offered," Carl said.

Pete wanted to ask how much ground they might cover the next day, but he hated to break in on the conversation, so he lay back and listened to the grasshoppers jumping in the dry grass. Above him an owl called to another owl in a neighboring tree and, after a pause, was answered. He wondered if the chicken hawk they'd watched earlier was also asleep in this big oak which spread like an umbrella above him. And how far was it to the running water he heard in the distance, and did the cows whose bells tinkled, ever so faintly, over the meadow come to that water? He hoped the three of them weren't in those cows' path but he didn't think of moving. It had been two days since he'd decided to run away, and he hoped he wasn't being hunted; but since there was noth-

42

ing he could do, he didn't worry about that either. They wouldn't think to look for him on this hillside. He couldn't remember ever feeling so at peace. Perhaps it was because he was finally on his way. Perhaps it was only the pain pills. Whatever the cause he was almost asleep when he heard his name.

"Pete. Pete, you'd better keep that shoulder covered or the cold will go spiraling in on those torn tendons so fast you won't know what hit you. Stay awake for a while or you'll roust us out at dawn. Tell me about yourself," Carl suggested.

"Not much to tell."

"Sure there is. Barney tells me you're heading for the Virgin Islands—sounds adventurous to me. Where do you come *from?*"

"A foster home, and they'll be glad to get rid of me," Pete mumbled, half asleep.

"Sure? I'd hate to stand trial for kidnapping—don't have the constitution." Carl bent toward the fire and lit a cigarette on a coal.

"Positive." But Pete was wide awake now. This conversation was taking a dangerous turn.

"You always live with these nice people?"

"No, I lived in another foster home for a long time— almost five years—they *were* nice."

"What happened? How come they didn't adopt you and everyone settle down? You can tell me to mind my own business, of course, and I might even do that—for a while."

Pete sighed. He noticed Barney leaning forward eagerly. He wanted to tell them both to mind their own business, but that would only delay the inevitable. He saw that in Carl's face.

"It's kind of hard to explain. They were always *going* to adopt me, but Roger—that was the guy—he drank— not all the time, but he'd go off on these bats—and the welfare got wind of it and they didn't like the idea and neither did Nita, his wife. Anyhow, before the adoption went through they split up and I landed back in juvenile. Not much more to say. Eventually I landed in this place where the boy my age couldn't stand me—because I made good grades, I guess. I *have* to make good grades. No one is going to put *me* through college."

"You sound a mite bitter, and I guess you have that right," Carl said quietly. "You've been around."

"I guess you could say that."

"Relax, show and tell's over. I don't intend to hassle you, Neptune."

"Me neither," Barney said very quietly.

"OK." Pete wondered about being called Neptune. Barney must have *also* said something about the marine biology. It was probably all right. This guy was curious, but he didn't seem like a meddler.

Softly, Carl began to whistle. It was an old cowboy tune, and Pete half listened, comforted that this night he could sleep without worrying about being hustled off a beach. And then he saw another beach, lined with palm trees, and he was walking up to a house set back from the sand, and his aunt was standing at the door, hesitating, and then she recognized him. The harmonica blended with the call of the owl and the sound of palm trees, and Pete drifted off to sleep.

Six

The sun warmed Pete's face and then seeped through the sleeping bag to his bad shoulder and arm, easing them. He'd put in a rough night, alternately falling asleep and then rolling over onto his usual sleeping position, which happened to be his right side, jumping up in pain and slipping back to sleep on his left side, only to roll and wake again.

He sat up. The field was alive with ground squirrels, beetles, and anonymous bugs of a thousand kinds. An anthill at his feet must send a million workers into the network covering his section of the meadow. He saw earwigs and grasshoppers the golden-green color of the grass itself. Both his foster fathers had pursued these bugs with all the insecticides at their disposal to give their flowers a chance, and yet here were insects and flowers living together. Poppies and lupines, buttercups and half a dozen flowers he couldn't name, bloomed in greater pro-

45

fusion than he'd *ever* seen in a garden. He wondered idly why people didn't simply plant wild flowers and let the bugs live, too.

He looked over the patch of field between him and the fire and saw that Barney and Carl were already at breakfast. The delicious aromas of coffee, chili beans, and hot rolls hung in the morning air. And yet he hesitated a minute, watching these two who had so haphazardly become a part of his life. On the whole, he was glad to be here with them—except for the torn tendons in his shoulder.

"Hey, Pete, better get up. We've got twenty minutes to hit the road. Burritos for breakfast." Carl's hair was wet, as if he might have bathed in the creek. He wore blue bermuda shorts and a matching short-sleeved shirt, at odds with his bushy beard, white legs, and cowboy boots.

Barney was eating a burrito, beans wrapped in an envelope of flour tortilla, while he peered over a road map. The beans kept dropping out on the map, and Barney would hastily retrieve them with a guilty look at Carl.

"Stop dropping beans on my map. You'll give it gas! And remember, Barney, we're stopping in Indio tonight. I've an old friend at The Garden of Allah who'll put us up. I'm open to reason tomorrow if we make decent time."

"I always wanted to see the Grand Canyon," Barney said.

"That's the other end of the state. Try some place along our route." Carl handed Pete a burrito as he came up to the fire.

"Why the dude clothes, Carl?" Pete asked.

46

"You ever been through the valley?— Nothing but reclaimed desert. Hot. Hot. Hot. How's the arm? You looked a little peaked."

"I found out I naturally sleep on my right side. I kept rolling over on the bad side."

"Ugh, that's too bad," said Barney.

"Maybe we should lay over a day?" Carl asked, impatience in his voice, and then gently, "We have six more days until I report in to the carnival at El Paso. I figure four days for the trip and two for calamities. I'm willing to say that arm is a calamity."

"No, I'm better off on the move. Keep my mind off it." Pete wasn't going to let himself in for any boy-scout treatment. "I'll take my pills, every one."

"Good boy. Indio's a long haul through. And I do want to make it and see a friend if we take off today." Carl started breaking camp. He had a peculiar, hopping walk, and his arms jerked along as if he were on marionette strings. Pete watched him as he ate a second burrito; the warm chili flavor, the flour tortillas, and the green peppers were the best breakfast he could remember. And it didn't need a plate.

"All set?" Carl said.

"How about Organ Pipe Cactus National Monument?" Barney asked.

"Will you *please* roll up that map? You have all day and half the night before we do any more deciding. It's possible—though that is about the world's ugliest spot."

Toward evening they pulled into Palm Springs. The sun was flamboyantly setting over waving palms and intriguing high walls, and shopkeepers were closing shutters and locking up.

Carl stopped the truck and dropped his hands on the wheel, saying nothing. Pete could see he was too tired to crawl out and find the coffee shop he needed. Pete himself was not sure he could walk at all. He'd taken two extra capsules so pain wouldn't make him ask to stop, and he felt like a rag doll. It wasn't a bad feeling, but walking was something else again. Besides, Barney was asleep on his good shoulder.

"I'll wait here, Carl."

"Not on your life. In half an hour you'll both need the john and in forty-five minutes you'll be thirsty. Come on, Barney, up and at 'em."

"Hey, where *are* we? It's beautiful." Barney yawned.

"Sunset in Palm Springs, the glamour capitol of the world. Pete and I just saw Humphrey Bogart—"

"No kidding?"

"Barney!"

"Oh, yeah, he's dead. Hey, doesn't Frank Sinatra live here?" Barney stared up and down the main street anxiously.

"You just might sit next to him at the coffee shop if you get a move on," Carl urged, waiting to lock up the car. "But don't string it out. We've more than an hour to Indio, and I told the guru we'd make it for dinner."

"Who's the guru?" Pete asked, stepping down from the truck gingerly. He had learned earlier that Carl had once been married to a snake charmer so it was possible his friends might be more interesting than most.

"One more question and you're hitchhikers. I will say, you've never met anyone like him. No, I won't bet on that. How you making it, underwater king?"

Pete nodded. He was wobbly but making it, a step

at a time. He felt clammy and was terribly grateful when they found an open coffee shop. Grateful too for the air conditioning. He ordered a cup of cocoa and hoped Carl didn't notice his hands shaking.

"This is just like any other restaurant, nothing special," Barney sniffed, looking around.

"And nobody famous?"

"There might be. I don't know every famous face in the world, do you, Carl?"

"Nope, I've been spared that." Carl gulped his coffee and apple pie and stood up.

Barney sucked the last of his milk shake dry so that every head swiveled their way.

"Maybe they think *you're* famous," Pete giggled.

"Maybe they're right," Barney slid off the high stool and followed Carl out the door, Charlie Chaplin style.

Pete giggled. At first it was funny and then he couldn't stop, even knowing his giggling came from the pills and the long trip more than from Barney's imitation. Something was wonderful, truly wonderful, and he couldn't stop laughing.

Still laughing and with tears rolling down his cheeks, he climbed in the truck.

"Watch it or you'll bang that shoulder," Barney said, subdued.

"Go to sleep. You'll be all right," Carl said and started the engine. He looked annoyed.

Pete was asleep before they hit the freeway.

It was well after dark by the time they turned up a long driveway and stopped before a massive wooden sign announcing THE GARDEN OF ALLAH. There was moonlight, and a grove of date palms standing out against the sky and against the high white wall circling the property made it look to Pete like the Taj Mahal. Behind the wall and through the palms he could see three enormous white buildings. A company of owls hooted and small bats rode the downdrafts of the night wind. There were no lights and a sense of desolation hung over The Garden of Allah.

"I never thought to see anything like this in my whole life. It's like—a mirage," Barney whispered.

"There've been times I wished it were," Carl muttered. "Used to be a date farm. Three hundred people were working and living here."

"What happened?" Pete asked.

"Went broke, of course." He honked his horn, shattering the fearful peace, frightening the owls.

"Why did it go broke?" Barney asked.

They waited.

"We should be riding up through the desert on camels," Barney said.

"Saddlesores," Carl muttered.

"Carl, maybe nobody's home?" Pete suggested.

Just then the heavy wooden gates started to squeak and, ever so slowly, swung open. Pete caught a glimpse of white-robed men pulling the gates.

Inside, a long path edged in abalone shells and ice plants led through the date grove. Date fronds and the fruit itself formed a thick matting under the trees so the white sand path gave the effect of a carpet leading up to the main house.

"It's spooky, so quiet," Barney said.

"That's what Larsen likes." Carl laughed.

"Oh, look!" Pete stared. There, on the top step of the

largest white mansion, his arms spread wide, stood the fattest man Pete had ever seen. He wore deep-orange silk robes, and his white hair hung below his shoulders.

"He's like an eagle ready to fly," Barney whispered.

"Yeah."

"He'd rather you thought he looked like Buddha," Carl whispered back, before calling out to the man. "Well, Larsen, why don't you move back to Hollywood and Vine, someplace accessible?"

"Because you never came to visit me there and here you are, my old friend. And your young visitors—we've been expecting you." Larsen had a deep voice, and he spoke slowly so that each word had its own emphasis. He took Pete's hand. "Ah, so tense, young man? You have no need to fear me," he said.

Then, turning to Barney, he took both hands, stared deeply into his eyes a few minutes and then gave him a great hug. "Welcome, welcome, friend!"

"This is a wonderful place!" Barney exclaimed, slowly extricating himself from the guru's arms.

"Loveliness is in the eye of the beholder. You have a generous spirit, young man."

"Don't you believe it. Barney here would bet his mother's trousseau—"

"Never mind, Carl. So too, did Paul, before he followed Jesus—"

"And Pete wants to live like Jacques Cousteau, chatting with dolphins in the middle of the Atlantic—"

"Ah, the benefits of television. Welcome, Barney and Peter. You travel in good company." The fat man bowed slightly and then turned and waddled slowly into the house.

Carl and Barney followed, and Pete trailed them slowly. He was furious that the guru made it sound like he was some little kid copying a television program. How could he know anything about either of them when all he'd done was take one look at Barney and decided he was some kind of saint, and one look at Pete and decided he wasn't worth bothering about? Hadn't even bothered to give him a hug, though *that* was a blessing. Pete heard them laughing inside and wondered what those three found to be so happy about.

They waited for Pete and then went through a huge central room that Larsen said had been the date-cutting room. It opened out onto other rooms nearly as big. Maybe they had been sorting and packing and storage rooms. Mexican rugs, colored pillows, and India spreads thrown over mattresses appeared to be the only furniture. Larsen flipped a switch, and the ceiling of the main room was bathed in soft light.

"Just finished the illumination today—for you," Larsen said.

"I'm impressed. Didn't think that crew of yours had it in them," Carl replied.

Larsen bowed.

"Barney, let's get out of here," Pete whispered.

"You crazy? This may be the most important thing that will ever happen to me. Relax, Pete. Did you ever meet *anyone* like this guy!"

Pete shrugged and poked along some distance behind the others. Finally they came to a long room with pale-blue banners hanging out along the two opposite walls. At the far end stood a fireplace, not in use on that warm evening. Tables were pushed together the length of the room, and Pete figured thirty or forty could eat there easily, though no one else was there at the moment. The room smelled of stew and lemon wax and Pete found the familiar odors comforting, something he could tie into. He'd felt terribly lonely ever since they met this guru, and it wasn't getting any better.

"It's like we were in King Arthur's Court—all by ourselves." Barney sounded rapt.

"Perhaps you remember from another incarnation," Larsen suggested. "What is your birth date?"

"Could you *really* tell about the past from a horoscope."

Barney had this habit of saying things that should be questions as absolute fact, and it annoyed Pete.

"Sometimes, Barney, sometimes."

"I was born October 2—how did you learn about telling horoscopes?" Barney looked mesmerized, and Pete turned away, disgusted.

"He was always good at reading the cards." Carl laughed.

The guru was nodding his head. "October 2—Libra—of course—one feels it in your vibration—the unstable moon—you must keep your control, and then there is nothing you cannot do. We will do a preliminary rough chart—tonight."

"I'll keep it all my life," Barney said.

The fat man smiled gently.

Later, after the dishes were cleared, they still sat at the long table. Larsen was marking a thick sheet of white cardboard with different colored pencils. There was a large circle intersected by lines and stars and moon. Around the outside of the circle were the different astrological signs. Larsen would stop occasionally and explain. The scales represented Barney's sign, Libra. Apparently Venus was his rising and the moon had a strong and possibly dangerous influence. This much Pete understood and wondered if Barney did. He just sat there looking up at the fat man like he worshipped him. You'd think this guy had just broken the track record for the mile or something.

Nevertheless, Pete couldn't help but wonder if the relation with the moon *did* explain Barney's gambling. He kept waiting for Larsen to ask what *his* sign was, but he acted as if Pete wasn't in the room unless he asked a question about Barney's chart. Not that Pete cared, but the guy *could* at least have been polite.

"Can you tell what I'll do—when I grow up?" Barney asked, with a queer tension in his voice.

"I would have to do a deeper study—this is only a rough—"

"You mean a fifty-buck horoscope rather than the twenty-five-dollar chart, don't you?" Carl asked sarcastically.

"Maybe I could work it out," Barney suggested, and the pleading in his voice made Pete's stomach churn.

"Oh, no!" Carl muttered.

"How did *you* get to live here in the first place?" Pete interrupted.

The fat man turned first to Carl and looked at him in silence, and then subjected Pete to the same scrutiny. Then he said quietly, "The Karma is good here, for those who stay."

"What he means is, the price is right. Free rent in return for repair work, restoration of this dump so the owner can sell it eventually, *isn't* that so?" Carl was working up to something. He sounded mad.

"The fox and the dove must live in peace, my dear Carl. One must not be afraid to walk away to the stars," Larsen said in the same gentle voice.

"Oh, come off it, Larsen, this beats being fat man in a sideshow, isn't that it?"

The two men looked at each other, narrowly and for a long time, and gradually the tenseness lessened and both began to smile. The guru laughed, and his laugh was low and joyous. Carl put out his hand, and the big man wrapped him in his arms.

"This life has its own kicks," he said.

"Just keep your sense of humor, and it's all right with me," Carl replied. "And let's wind up the astrology for tonight. You two could both use some sleep, and I want a chance to gossip with Larsen, here. Neptune, don't forget your pill."

"But—my chart?"

The guru put an arm around Barney's shoulder. "I must consider. You shall have the chart in the morning."

Barney and Pete had little to say to each other. They lay in the room beyond the dining room listening to the older men talking about their carnival days when Carl had been the barker for Larsen's act. Soon the voices blurred for Pete. He knew it must be the medicine, and he was grateful for a soft bed. Perhaps this night he would be able to sleep.

Pete opened his eyes to morning. Outside he heard the birds and the peculiar sea noise of date palms slapping, like a surf lapping the beach. Then he gradually made out voices, angry voices.

"But, Carl, I *have* to know my future. You just don't understand! Pete can keep you awake, and Lily won't mind. I'll be in Florida by the time she expects me, and she said I could get there any way I wanted. That's what she *said*."

"Then Lily can let you come back."

"No."

"Look. Don't get tough with me. If you want that preliminary horoscope chart this morning, you are coming with us and that is final. I told Larsen that I was responsible to your grandmother. Now get your gear in that truck."

Pete didn't hear Barney's reply but in a moment a door slammed. He shuddered. This could be one long road to El Paso! *If* Barney even came. Very reluctantly Pete crawled out of bed.

Seven

Barney and Carl bickered through Arizona and into New Mexico about whether Larsen was a carny with a new graft or a holy man whom Carl was afraid to face. Two days after they left The Garden of Allah, Barney was still planning to return when he'd found out the exact hour of his birth. He *did* say he'd wait until he made the fare back if they could get jobs in the carnival. But neither Pete nor Barney had yet worked up the courage to ask Carl what the chances of their getting a job might be. And they never *would* get the chance if Barney didn't stop arguing with Carl. Pete was tired of listening, and he couldn't understand *why* it was so important to either of them what the other thought of Larsen, though he personally agreed with Carl.

"Listen," Carl was saying late one afternoon as they sped along an almost deserted highway. "Listen, Barney, if you really cared about this astrology, you would have been gung ho to find out what *our* signs are. You'd have wanted to know what the stars had to say about Pete and me, and you haven't so much as asked our birth dates. So it isn't the astrology that's got you hooked—"

"I keep telling you, and you just don't hear, Carl. In the first place, neither of you believe, so why should I push you? But, mainly, I just want to know if there's anything I can do to *control* my future *at all*. Pete knows what he wants to do. You seem to like your life. But I'm afraid that—" Barney's voice trailed off. Pete kept waiting for him to say more, but the silence hung on and on in the cab of the truck.

"Afraid of *what?*" Carl asked.

"Never mind."

"All right! If you want to be the big mystery boy and bring up fears and leave them hanging, go ahead. Larsen might be willing to coax you, but not me." Carl's hands gripped the steering wheel.

"At least he's a guy who's not afraid to show he likes a guy, and probably if he feels like laughing or crying he does that, too. That's why he might be able to help me." Barney sounded weary, like the fire had gone out of the argument.

"The ideal father figure," Carl muttered.

That was an interesting comment, Pete thought. Barney had said during lunch that arguing with Carl was just like trying to talk an ounce of sense into Lily and saved him the bother of being homesick. Maybe he *was* homesick. Strange. Pete felt he could spend the rest of his life in this truck cab, seeing the country, even listening to the two of them arguing so long as he could dream by himself. Even the Virgin Islands began to be heat haze in his mind, along with the aunt he could neither forget nor quite get clear in his mind. He couldn't remember ever feeling so free, ever enjoying himself as much as he had these last few days. Of course, he supposed Barney had more at home *to* miss.

It was late that night when they pulled into a field outside of Las Cruces. They'd been hunting for a suitable place for two hours and hadn't found a thing with a speck of privacy. A person could see five miles back from the barbed wire fences shining in the moonlight, five miles back on either side of the road. Back over short stubble grass and herds of steer. It was a dry desolate country, eerie with the cry of the coyote and alive with the light of a million fireflies. Locoweed rolled across the fields, gathering other clumps, sometimes growing to a great ball that looked like a slow tornado, or so Barney said.

The countryside continued barren, and Carl was looking for rolling hillsides and big trees and water, so it was well after 10 P.M. before they compromised on a creek lined with cottonwood trees that wound down away from the road into a triangular hollow, enough so they wouldn't be plagued with headlights from the highway all night, but not what you'd call a valley. The fence at this point was old and broken so they figured this was deserted land and they moved in, gratefully, for no one had eaten since noon. They'd been lucky to find any water at all.

They moved easily into their usual division of labor. Pete started dinner while Barney and Carl went for wood and the water they'd driven so far to find. Pete was exhausted and his arm ached, but it was comforting to stumble through his chores, to know that Barney and Carl needed him and he could come through.

59

The far-off cry of coyotes cut through the night, carried by the sharp wind, a stinging hot wind that cut through Pete's Levi jacket and made him question whether it was really safe to start a fire. Suppose it got out of control? But when the fire was started with the only wood they could find, branches torn from the cottonwoods by some previous wind, it smoked and burned only long enough to heat lukewarm the canned beans and Franco-American spaghetti, then blew to an enormous geyser of green-gray smoke, and died.

"Snakebite country," Carl muttered, sniffing the air. He had a cold and, despite the heat, sat wrapped in an old wool army blanket. Carl wouldn't have nylon or drip-dries near him, figuring that man was compatible with natural fibers and set up negative energy with synthetics. "I'm gonna turn in as soon as I grab some coffee out of that thermos, which we carry for just this kind of calamity."

"All right, I still say it's hardly worth making coffee every day so you drink it one day out of seven. And you know what Larsen said about coffee being the enemy of tranquillity."

"Listen, Barney, one thing you learn on the road, a hot cup of Java can make the difference between a good life and some damn miserable times. Coffee, a down sleeping bag, and a few traveler's checks, and don't you forget it."

"Where are you going to bed down?" Pete asked quickly. He'd heard enough about Larsen for one day. The idea of coyotes was unsettling, he hated snakes, and he'd rather be near Barney and Carl this night. They were about the only targets as far as he could see across this flat, windswept land, and coyotes or snakes could hardly miss them no matter how far away they might be. And he'd seen steer, heard their low and their bells, and while he had nothing against them, he didn't want to get stepped on, either.

"Down by the cottonwoods, no closer to the creek than need be because of mosquitoes and snakes, looks to be about as good as we can do. But we can unload the truck and use that if you'd rather."

Barney groaned.

Pete shrugged.

"Thank God, you're lazy," Carl called back over his shoulder as he unrolled his sleeping bag. "Hey, Mackerel, tomorrow we'd best have a medic take a look at that arm again. Just to be on the safe side."

"Hey, no, it's doing fine. No way," Pete said, thinking of the fifteen bucks the doctor charged last time. To say nothing of ten for X rays. He rather liked it when Carl called him Mackerel, said he was returning to his spawning ground by going to the Virgin Islands. Not that he'd ever really been there before, but he liked the idea of going back, anyhow.

"You were the guy who told me a marine biologist had to be in perfect physical shape—don't cop out now."

Pete didn't say anything more. He'd learned it was easier to do what Carl wanted. Sometimes he forgot, anyway. Pete looked over to where Carl lay rolled up in his sleeping bag, curled cocoonlike, the red coal of a cigarette the only evidence he was still awake. Pete looked at Barney, who shook his head.

"I think it would be better if *you* asked him," Barney whispered. "You get along better."

61

"But you know him better—"

"Yeah, but he might figure I want a job in the carnival for travel money back to The Garden of Allah and then neither of us would have a chance."

Pete considered this. Carl *might* refuse them jobs if he worried about Barney heading back. And he owned two booths and had been with the show a long time, so his word would kill their chance. Pete knew that even if he could take off the sling, there would be very few jobs he could get or do with the dislocated shoulder. If he didn't get a job, he'd never get beyond Miami.

"All right," he said. "I'll ask him—tomorrow. Just take it easy with Carl until I get the chance."

"He probably wishes he'd left us home," Barney said sadly.

Home. Barney was using that word again, and it wasn't one Pete liked to think about. Barney didn't even have to worry about a job when Lily would eventually see that he got home. Pete had never had what he'd *really* call a home, but there was nothing like a wind-raked New Mexico plain to make one sound desirable.

There were supposed to be lots of poisonous snakes in New Mexico. But they slept at night, didn't they? He'd read somewhere that rattlers didn't. Maybe he should ask Barney? But Barney didn't know fact one about either fish or animals, let alone snakes. He should just make sure the sleeping bag was closed. A few minutes later he turned his back to the wind and pulled out a harmonica and began to play softly.

Neither Barney nor Carl complained, so Pete played a long while, trying to listen for night noises and trying to drown them out at the same time. He had a curious empty feeling and the harmonica was soothing. Finally he fell asleep with the harmonica still at his lips.

But he slept restlessly and so, just before dawn, he heard something moving in the underbrush, coming toward their camp. He broke into a cold sweat but could not move, could not force any sound from his dry throat. At least it wasn't snakes. Too heavy. Maybe robbers. Then he heard a bell and knew they'd been invaded by steers, by the herd that he'd heard lowing across the mesquite earlier. They must have come to the creek for water. Carl said steers were placid and wouldn't bother a man.

Still, he'd hate to be stepped on by mistake. He was about to call Barney when he heard one of the cattle pawing the ground and breathing in curious short snorts. Sounded mad. Not very placid. Pete was wide awake now, sniffing the fresh dung and hunting for the great dark hulks of cattle against the dark night.

He saw the animal, saw him separate himself from what must be the others and, slowly at first, then picking up speed, deliberately lunge at the truck! The dull crunch was expected, no longer surprising.

"Carl," Pete warned, in the split second between the crunch of horns against metal and the cry of the steer. A horrible, high-pitched, pain-crazed cry. Not at all the low roar bulls are supposed to have, Pete thought. More like a peacock. Gradually diminishing, like a siren, as the great animal lumbered away across the plain. The others, there must have been about half a dozen more, followed their leader.

"What *was that?* Watch it, stay put while I check it out."

Pete could see nothing but the beam of Carl's flashlight, making arcs and finally coming to rest on the front of his truck. He could still hear the hoofbeats, gradually quieting with the distance they were putting between themselves and the camp. Dust from their retreating hoofbeats settled over everything.

"What happened?" Barney asked quietly.

"Fool steer's gone into the radiator," Carl yelled, as if it were Barney's doing.

"There must have been at least half a dozen," Pete heard himself say, surprised that he had any idea of the number. He pulled on Levi's and shoes and started rolling up his sleeping bag before he thought to take his flashlight and stand with Carl and Barney, staring at the crumpled fender and grill and sprung hood of their truck.

"Think they'll be back?" Barney asked in a whisper.

"But why would he go for the car—truck must have just gotten in their way," Pete murmured.

"He got the radiator. There's no fixing that one." Carl whistled, a long sharp question, as they watched the water in the beam of the flashlight dripping into a murky puddle on the dry grass. They stood there shivering, watching the water until the flow had stopped and large drops splattered on the puddle, making more noise than the flow.

"Think they'll come back?"

"Not for fifty years, anyhow." Carl laughed. "Well, better get a fire going. I need some coffee this morning."

It was still pitch black, but no one argued.

"Hit the radiator and smashed it to smithereens," Barney said, as if he were already telling someone who hadn't been present. The car shifted, settling.

"Stumbled over the truck is more likely. Well, that shoots today and God knows how many more. I knew this

64

luck was too good. Just couldn't see *how* it was going to blow, but I knew it would, always does." Carl snapped off the flashlight. Gradually the anger went out of his face and then the worry, and pretty soon he was laughing. Carl had a low deep laugh that sounded to Pete like he was happy all the way down to his toes.

"Wait till I tell them at a garage how *this* radiator got busted—Barney, how much you want to bet we find *anyone*, anyone at all who believes us? A buck? Pete, you're tighter with your money—fifty cents?"

Pete was hurt to be called tight with his money. He wanted to say something about the doctor bills that Barney hadn't faced, but then he didn't, he just nodded.

"Yeah, fifty cents."

"What I want to know is *how* we're going to get this piece of junk to the garage?" Barney asked, ignoring the bet altogether.

"There goes the last of the water. Maybe this will be the only spot on the desert to grow wild flowers, commemorating the death of a car. Funny you should ask that about getting the car to a shop, Barney, because it brings to mind another time I was stuck way out like this and what do you think I went and done? Car threw a rod that time and had to be towed, though, of course, there wasn't a tow truck inside of ten miles."

"You sent someone name of Barney to hoof it to the nearest town, of course."

Carl didn't say a word, just raised one eyebrow high. "No, no, no."

"Me neither!" Pete said definitely.

"Well, sir, what I done the other time was to simply harness two cows to the front and off they went, cowbells

65

ringing, right down the road and me with the switch walkin' beside them. You should of seen the looks on faces when cars passed us, and the shoutin' and whistlin', and none of it bothered those two cows or the car. Cows kept right on chewing their cud."

"If there's anything worse than a poor liar, I don't know what it is, do you, Pete?"

"Yeah, a bull with a busted head, Barney, but that's the only thing."

"OK, wise guys. So what do you suggest?"

"We make a fire and have some breakfast first, and by that time there'll be *some* cars along the highway," Pete offered timidly.

"No romance in your soul," Carl muttered and winked back at Pete as he started toward the stand of cotton-woods for firewood.

Eight

They sat in a corner of the restaurant, the A-1 Truck Stop, El Paso. It had taken a day and a half to get the new radiator installed because they'd had to get it from a junkyard, so Carl had been driving most of the last twenty-four hours in order to make the 7 P.M. check-in deadline at the carnival. He'd make it, just under the wire, but now he sat hunched over the table, his eyes drained with fatigue, picking at his custard pie.

The two boys watched him silently. This could be the last meal they'd ever share with Carl. He might say good-bye as they walked out the door. In a way he'd already left, Pete thought. This man with the short, neatly trimmed beard and hair, the shoestring tie and summer jacket, was hardly the Paul Bunyan mountain man they'd ridden across country with.

A week ago Pete hadn't known Carl, and he'd gotten along. He hadn't even liked Carl at first. He still planned to ask about the job, but he didn't think there was much hope. He hadn't dared while it was touch-and-go whether they'd get here on time. He'd planned on working his way across and here he'd gotten a ride halfway so there were no grounds for complaint. But that wasn't it, either. The truth was that he hated the idea of never seeing Carl again. He'd miss him. Carl was a comfortable kind of person to be with.

Pete looked around, waiting for Carl to look a little less tired and preoccupied so he could ask about a job. The restaurant was filled with truckers, big men in Levi's and dirty shirts rolled to the elbow, bent over the counter, most of them eating steak and French fries, laughing and swapping stories, flirting with a waitress who must be at *least* fifty years old. They met the same old friends at different stops. *They* knew where they'd be and what they'd be doing next week. It wouldn't be a bad life.

"Yeah, look at them," Barney said bitterly. "Dumb oxen following the road day after day, saddlesore and half-blind from watching road signs. Snow-blind from blizzards half the year and worrying about flaking out from heat prostration the rest of the time. To say nothing of dodging drunks. Probably be just my luck to end up at that counter in a few years."

"Could do worse, you know," Carl said quietly.

"That's all you know."

"Is that what you want to be, a truck driver?" Pete asked curiously. Barney never said anything about his future except that he worried about it—or the present either, except that he didn't like school.

"And go over an embankment before I'm forty, like my

68

old man? You must be kidding! Makes my skin crawl every time I even get *near* a bunch of truckers. But I keep seeing me driving in my dreams, and I have this funny feeling, like it's my fate." Barney's face was white, drained.

"So *that's* the big fear. I would never have guessed it in a hundred years," Carl said.

"Do you—is that why the astrology?" Pete asked.

"I guess. Maybe I can find out if I have a chance."

"You're nothing but a monkey on a string, is that it?" Carl snorted. "Aren't you copping out a little early?"

"If I knew what I wanted to be, like Pete—"

"He's likely to change his mind half a dozen times before he settles down—at least I hope he'll feel he can. How about it, Pete?" Carl finished his pie and signaled the waitress for a second cup of coffee.

"Still," Barney said, and Pete could see he was not convinced.

"Thanks a lot." Pete shrugged. So Carl hoped he'd change his mind. He wouldn't *ever* but no sense in making a hassle when everyone was so tired. People who just drifted into something like Carl, always seemed to think other guys didn't know their minds. Carl probably didn't even believe he'd *get* to the Virgin Islands.

"Relax, Mackerel. I'm not putting down marine biology. I'm just hoping you'll be open enough if you want— if you find your interests changing—that—same as I hope for Barney—you'll count yourself as more important—" Carl broke off and glanced at his watch. Pete looked across the table at Barney, who nodded slowly.

"Say, Carl, is there any chance—" Pete had practiced a week, but he still couldn't complete the sentence.

"We have an appointment in half an hour. So eat up."

Pete shook his head. "Where's the appointment, Carl?"

"Edge of town." Carl smiled.

"Bet you a buck he means that's a good spot for hitching?"

"Is there any chance Barney and I could work for the carnival? We'd do anything." Pete hated the plaintive tone in his voice. But at least it was out. They'd been planning to ask since they left California, and finally he'd managed. Pete waited.

"And Barney, I'll bet you'll end up broke before you hit the Louisiana border if you don't quit laying wager on every sentence I speak. Haven't you noticed your odds are pretty poor?"

"Come off it, Carl. I've been watching you playing with that pie, worrying it to death with your fork for the last fifteen minutes, trying to get up the courage to tell us to flake off."

That's why he hasn't answered me, Pete thought, because he doesn't have the guts.

"Oh, just goes to show how bad a gambling man he'd make, right Pete? And don't think I didn't hear your question, Mackerel, or haven't heard the two of you whispering for days about when to ask me about working for the carnival. Of all the cowards—well, it so happens I checked with the boss last night, and he happened to mention being short a couple of roughies, and I had inklings you might want to apply for the job—since you're headed in that direction—just one thing, Barney, you go on to Florida before any heading back to get the divine light from Larsen—if you get the job. Agreed?"

"Wow!"

"That means double fare but OK," Barney said with less enthusiasm.

"But who'd hire *me* when they see this sling?" Pete asked ruefully.

"Take the sling off until you've got the job. *Then,* an arm in a sling just might make a concession look honest—never can tell."

"You mean like crippled beggars?" Barney asked, still somewhat subdued by his promise.

"Want to give it a try, Pete?" Carl asked.

"Sure, Ill try. Got nothing to lose, might as well."

"Of course, a dislocated shoulder isn't in there with leprosy or a peg leg, but it might squeeze a tear from *some* marks."

"That sounds cruel," Pete said.

"Poor folks can't be squeamish," Carl replied, signaling for the check.

The carnival lay near the edge of town. At the end of the bus line. At a shopping center near the last housing development. They passed posters all the way out, congratulating drivers on going the right way to the carnival.

Carl parked on the far edge of an almost empty parking lot, and they stood looking out across the flat dry land to the weather-beaten orange, yellow, and tan tents, all flying colorful balloons, flags, and rope-pole disks that creaked as they twirled in the evening wind. The wind was hot and dusty. And rock music drifted back from the carnival. They could smell buttered popcorn, beer, and hot dogs. As they watched, the lights went on, softening and exciting the carnival village. To one side of the show lay the house trailers and trucks where the crew lived, circled like covered wagons against an ambush.

"Isn't it beautiful? Oh, God, I hope they take me," Pete said.

"When I was a kid, I was always afraid the gypsies in carnivals would come and steal me." Barney looked around uneasily.

"I wouldn't have minded," Pete muttered.

"Be sure you take off that sling," Carl called back over his shoulder.

It was dusk, and the early customers were drifting toward the lights and the ticket booths. Pete looked at half a dozen boys in a group, about his and Barney's age, and felt superior. They were just kids going to spend their money, but he and Barney could get on the inside, might even be working here.

"Maybe we should have gone on," Barney whispered.

"You're crazy!" He hurried to catch up with Carl.

"Hi, Mike," Carl said casually to an old man in the ticket booth outside a sideshow. "How's it going?"

"Can't complain. Wouldn't do me any good. *You're* a sight for sore eyes, boy; when did you get in?"

"Within the hour. Stopped and saw Larsen in Indio."

"How is the old devil? He still have that Garden of Allah of his? I keep telling the boss, religion's where it's at. Gal came around and wanted to run an I Ching parlor—boss turned her down, but then he had some second thoughts and he says he'll try her out if she comes back." Mike shook his head.

"Larsen's got that old date farm looking pretty shipshape. He gave me a message for you. 'Tell that devil to come.' Just that." Carl stepped to the side of the booth to let the line pass. Mike sold a batch of tickets and then turned back to them.

72

"And I will, just as soon as we go into winter quarters. I miss that old shyster, I really do. These buddies of yours?" The ticket taker peered intently, and Pete squirmed in much the same way as he had under Larsen's scrutiny. Did all carnies give everyone the evil eye?

"Is Mr. Larsen a good friend of yours?" Barney asked eagerly.

"Mr. Larsen, how formal can you get!"

"Later. Later. The boss in?" Carl pushed Pete and Barney through the crowd.

The boys followed Carl into a barrage of twirling lights and music and barkers. The carnival was just getting under way. Some of the stands they passed were already playing. The colors, stands, and music seemed to Pete to be all run together, as if he were standing in the middle of a light show. The field had been watered down earlier as a fire precaution and, all around them, steam was rising in the hot night, adding to the feeling that he was walking through a dream.

It was early, and the crowd was just gathering. Young couples, gangs of boys and girls, families, loners—all had an expectant, faintly bewildered look, as if they had come to have a good time but didn't quite know where to begin. Pete felt the same way himself, only with him the joy was waiting on a job. He tried to see himself working in each of the concessions: the freak show, an animal house that advertised for all comers to wrestle with a chimpanzee, or maybe one of the stand-up eating wagons they passed as they went down a main runway toward the shooting gallery. Over to one side he saw the rides: a Ferris wheel, a merry-go-round, the Whip, Loop-o-plane, and a Mad Mouse. They did not turn toward these but

73

continued straight toward the circle of house trailers. Carl waved and called to almost every operator they passed, but he did not stop and did not introduce them. Maybe he was waiting until he saw if they'd be hired?

"Later," Carl said tersely when Barney wanted to stop and try his luck with the paper targets in the shooting gallery. "We can fool around later, after we see the big man."

Carl walked rapidly, chain smoking, his face tense as they made their way through the crowd in front of the sideshows and crossed a littered field to the trailers. One door opened and three young women in sequinned evening dresses, with tall plumes in their hair, hurried toward the midway. Pete could hear voices and the laughter from a television show. The smell of frying meat hung over the circle of trailers. A baby was crying. Over to one side stood the carnival trucks.

Carl knocked on the aluminum door of the biggest and newest trailer.

"All right, what's wrong now?" a voice called out.

"It's just me, Sam, Carl Bonner."

"Well, why didn't you say so? Come on in! You're a sight for sore eyes—you can't believe the things have gone wrong today—you just would not *believe* it—" A husky bald man, middle-aged, with a ready smile and sad eyes, stood in the doorway shaking his head. He threw his arms around Carl and smiled at Barney and Pete over Carl's shoulder. Still smiling, his eyes narrowed, and Pete had the definite impression they were being sized up.

"Looks like this will be a good spot," Carl said.

"Can't complain for a still show. But it won't hurt my feelings when we hit the county fair circuit in a couple of weeks and I don't have to sweat out each and every night.

74

Oh, it hasn't been too bad—weather's liable to turn though. Look like the makings of a thunderhead to you?"

"Does smell like rain."

"Afraid of that. Well, are you coming back to us, Carl?"

"Sure I am. Looks like my relief is out for the season. Bleeding ulcers, so I'm back to run my booth. Brought you a couple of helpers—"

"Looks to me like you brought me another headache. All right, kids, suppose you give me one good reason I should hire you. Two good reasons. Kids are coming on the lot looking for jobs every day. Why should I choose you?" The man hitched his thumbs in his suspenders, rocked on his heels and waited, his eyes on Pete.

"On the lot, on the lot," a hard voice echoed from inside the trailer.

"What's *that?*" Barney jumped.

"Just Joe. Don't mind him. Can't keep his mouth shut."

"Joe's a parrot," Carl said gently. "How goes it, Joe?"

"Sight for sore eyes," squawked the parrot.

"Might as well come on in and say hello." Once the trailer door was closed, the big man let the red-and-yellow parrot out of his cage and the bird perched on Carl's shoulder. Carl stroked his wings but did not say anything else to him.

"Never did you see anything like it—well, outside of being Joe's friend's friend, what do you have to offer, boy?" His voice was friendlier, now that they were in the trailer.

"I—well, you must need more hands when you start county fairs, and I can make change and ballyhoo and I'm pretty good on the harmonica and—I'll do anything to come." Pete flushed. He'd blown his cool, sounded like a begging kid. He saw that his hands were shaking and shoved them under the table. And he couldn't handle half the jobs he'd probably have to do with the bad shoulder. He should have specified *what* work he could handle.

"That bad, huh? Trouble at home?" the boss asked.

"Orphan, no trouble," Pete said. He wasn't going into another spiel and make things worse.

"I'll sign for him, and I have the grandmother's note for Barney," Carl said. "I can use one of them in my booth."

"At least *that's* in your favor. Why didn't you say so in the first place. How about you, Red? You as husky as you look?"

Barney rolled up one shirt sleeve and flexed his muscle. "I can fix motorcycles, too," he added.

"Sight for sore eyes. Sight for sore eyes," the parrot shrilled. Everyone laughed.

"Well, I guess if Joe likes you, you're in. You have any trouble with nausea or allergies to popcorn or hot dogs?"

Barney shook his head, smiling for the first time.

"Then we'll try you on a food wagon. It's simple enough, popping corn, sticking hot dogs, making batter, and waiting on customers. Minimum wages to start and maybe a percentage of sales if you work out, no overtime, everyone helps with the teardown and setting up in a new town. Three square meals, which is more than you'll get in most carnivals. Pete, the same deal for you except that you'll work in one of Carl's concessions—and you can sleep under the trucks with the rest of the young guys."

"I'll put him in the dime throw."

The big man nodded. "He should handle the dimes all right. You can start tomorrow night, boys, but the first hint of trouble—the law, drugs, liquor, or girls—and you're out on your ear. No second chance in my show. OK, here's some passes. Go out and have yourselves a time, probably the only night you'll see it from the outside. You're dismissed, go, and leave a couple of old men to catch up on their gossip. You don't need permission from Carl. I'm your boss now, and don't you forget it." The big man took the parrot off Carl's shoulder and put him back in his cage. The bird ruffled his feathers and nipped at his owner but said nothing further.

"Before the bird has an accident," the boss added, opening the trailer door for Pete and Barney.

"How do you like *that*—Lily signed an affidavit so I could work here—before we left, and Carl never said *one* word," Barney said when they stood in the dark outside the ring of warm trailers. Fireflies darted around windows, and next door the carnival ran loud and bright, putting them in a silent black pocket of the summer night.

Pete couldn't stop shaking. He didn't trust himself to say anything. Barney seemed to think they'd been hired. Maybe it had been in the works since they left Sebastopol, but, though he remembered Barney being hired, he wasn't sure about himself.

"Did he promise to pay me, too?" he managed finally.

"*Carl* pays you. Lucky you, working for Carl. Oh, you're a sight for sore eyes. A sight for sore eyes," he mimicked the parrot, poking Pete in the ribs.

"Hey, stop it."

"And did you ever see the likes of such a trailer?— deep red wall-to-wall rugs and brown leather overstuffed

77

couch and velvet wallpaper. Biggest trailer I've ever seen, too. Bet it would take three spaces easy in that Sebastopol court. Wait till Lily hears about this—it'll blow her mind. Hey, did you see a phone booth? I promised her I'd call when we got to El Paso and let her know what next. Hey, come *to*." Barney snapped his fingers in Pete's face.

"We really made it. We really *made* it! Barney! We're carnies! It's like a miracle." Pete grabbed Barney's arm.

"Hey, stop, you're shaking like a leaf. Calm down. Haven't you ever gotten a job before? Minimum pay is not much, you know, this is no great deal. We'd make more doing dishes in the A-I Truck Stop. It's just that Carl could get us on here, and they're going our way. No big thing. You're the one keeps his cool, remember?" Barney took out his dice and began to roll them in his left hand.

Pete dropped his hand to his side and stared at Barney. He's afraid, he thought. Maybe he's right, but he's also afraid. What was it he'd said about all the furniture and the red rug? Pete tried to recall the trailer, but he didn't see anything but the parrot perched quietly on Carl's shoulder. He wouldn't know the boss if he saw him on the lot. It was all a blank. The only other time he'd ever gone blank was at track meets.

"I guess," he said slowly, "I guess this is the best thing that's ever happened to me."

Barney shrugged and started toward the lights. "Let's find a phone. And don't get too optimistic, Pete. The vibrations around here don't feel all that good to me."

Vibrations had become one of Barney's favorite words, and it reminded Pete that Barney wanted the money to return to The Garden of Allah, which was another problem.

Nine

The next afternoon Pete and Carl walked slowly down the center midway toward Carl's dime-pitch booth. The carnival was open, but there were few customers yet and booth operators leaned listlessly over their counters. Men with wide rakes rather aimlessly rounded up paper cups, beer cans, butts, and greasy papers. Stale smells, slightly nauseating, hung over the grounds. From time to time Carl would stop and introduce Pete, but no one seemed to care about meeting him and acted as if they had last spoken with Carl a few minutes before. Pete envied Barney who didn't have to start in the food wagon until evening and had gone off somewhere. It had all seemed so different last night.

"How come everyone is so blah—I don't know—like they don't give a damn?" Pete asked.

"Oh?" Carl was watching two young girls in short skirts ambling along ahead of them.

"Last night everyone was so friendly, so vivo, I don't know." Pete wished he'd kept his mouth shut. Carl had a habit of looking down at his custom-made boots, as if for reassurance, before he made one of his put-down cracks, and he was doing it now.

"Well, you know how glad-handed you feel when you get up in the morning? These people *worked* until two, and they're just on their first cup of coffee now. Give them a couple of hours to get with it. Incidentally, you were flying pretty high yourself last night. Didn't know you had so much whoopee in you." Carl gave Pete a playful jab at the ribs.

Pete didn't answer. What was there to say when everybody was so surprised if he wasn't the world's number one stick-in-the-mud?

"Oh, come on, Neptune, cheer up, or I'll wish I'd kept Barney," Carl said as they turned toward the booth. "There's old Clarence, just doing what comes naturally. Sleeping." Carl leaned over the side and pulled on the white goatee of an old man who slumped on a kitchen chair, a straw hat over his face, then ducked down behind the counter and winked at Pete. The booth was in yellow and orange stripes, freshly painted, and one of the largest on the midway, Pete noticed with a kind of pride. The same feeling made him realize that Carl had chosen *him*.

"Only one man in the world that mean," the hat replied. "And he wears dude boots."

"Clarence, the marks are stealing the glasses, taking them off by the shopping-bag load," Carl said, jumping over the side of the booth and pulling Pete after him. "Wake up and look what I brought."

"Welcome to 'em." The man had not moved except to fold gnarled hands over his stomach. He was a small wiry man who wore cowboy clothes, leather chaps over his Levi's, leather vest over pinstriped shirt. His high-heeled boots were western, gaudier than Carl's, but as elegantly made and as highly polished. Carl tapped one toe lightly with his heel, and Clarence bolted up.

"Leave be!" he said sternly. And then, "So here's the banty with the damaged wing—glad to meet you, boy, but you're in poor company."

"You look just like Buffalo Bill." Pete stared at the flowing white hair, the goatee and bushy-browed blue eyes, and felt again the rough, worn cover of the biography he'd taken out over and over until the librarian had to let someone else have it.

"Pure accident," Carl muttered. "He takes Bill Cody's picture to the barber. Just happens to have it in his wallet."

"Bill Cody would never have showed up two days late without a word to let a man know." The old man stood with his knobby hands hooked in his vest pockets, his body taut, his eyes angry. "I been running both booths by myself except for that moron you hired—alone, to speak truth—since your relief took sick."

"I asked the boss to tell you. A steer butted my radiator, and we had to wait two days for a replacement." Carl's voice was tired, sad.

"That so? Could have phoned me. A steer? Well, that figures, all right. Well—I'd better check on the other booth. Someone has to attend to business."

Carl stood looking after his jointee as the man stalked down the midway, flicking a cane.

81

"He sounded mad," Pete suggested.

"We've worked together a long time, maybe too long. He's put out that I called the boss rather than him. Protocol. Maybe he heard I was on the lot last night but I was too dead beat to start—Well, are *you* ready to work?"

"Sure."

"All right, you can start by cleaning the display glasses. Then wash the ashtrays, vases, maybe the cookie jars, and dust off the rest of the stuff. Then you might get some more stock from the trailer—here's the key— and if there's time, the outside of the booth could use a dusting down if there aren't customers milling around."

"But when do I learn the game?" Carl sounded like some teacher outlining the semester's work.

"Tell the truth, you don't need to. It's the customers going to be tossing those little dimes, Neptune. What you do is get them to stop and throw their dimes at *our* booth rather than the one down the way. Then, when your come-on hooks them, all you do is stand here with one hand out for the cash and the other passing out change. If a *guy* gets close, you say darn the wind or that would have got a cookie jar sure. If a *girl* tosses, tell her how pretty she looks when she gets mad. The big thing is making the guy and girl look good to each other. That's about all there is to it. The only *real* mistake you can make is pocketing cash."

"Thanks a lot. You don't trust anyone, do you?"

"Touchy. Come on! Look, I can't fight with both you and Clarence. You're a smart boy, good student, you have to stop being so everlastingly vulnerable. Here's your change apron. Tonight we'll give you twenty-five dollars in dimes for starters. After, you can make change with whatever folding money the marks have given you. When the dimes are gone, you turn in the cash to Clarence or me, and we'll exchange it for dimes and you start all over. OK? Good, and one more thing, if change drops on the floor here, just leave it. We rake it up at the end of the night. Easier that way." Carl stopped, ran one hand through his shorter hair and pulled uneasily on his trimmed beard. "Anything else?"

Pete shook his head. Carl's crack about keeping his hand out of the till still rankled.

"You'll do all right." Carl looked around the booth. "I've seen cleaner. Well, I'll be back. Going to soothe the tiger." He winked and jumped over the counter.

"Dude boots is right," Pete muttered. He looked around the booth and felt better. This was one of the big booths on the midway, open on all four sides to customers. There'd be two or three working, or should be for such a big booth. Carl had said that thirty or forty percent was returned in merchandise, almost entirely in glasses, so that a family could leave with a shopping bag full of prizes. Pete remembered that for a while he'd had a glass he'd won and drinking out of it had always brought back the thrill of winning. So it ought to be fun working this booth.

By midnight Pete was passing out the change automatically. It had become a game to see how much he could get a customer to spend, a game the marks seemed to enjoy as much as he did.

"Money's just an exchange for life is all," Clarence said at one point. He and Clarence worked the booth alone for most of the night, while Carl and another guy worked the other booth Carl owned.

When he had a moment to look out at the rest of the carnival it was a jumble: a light show; a maze of coins jingling as they changed hands; brightly lit rides twirling through the summer night; customers standing six deep in front of his own booth, waiting patiently to throw dimes for glasses they could buy in the five-and-ten-cent stores, or for the grand prizes of lanterns and lamps, which no one had won so far. Pete caught the momentum, and he laughed joyously as he egged the customers on.

"You *are* with it for a first-nighter." Clarence nodded approvingly.

"Didn't know I was such a ham myself." He wished Barney and Carl could see him. They wouldn't think he was an introvert.

A girl his own age came up and, without a word, lay down a dollar bill. She was a pretty girl with long black hair; rosy cheeks, and a teasing way of narrowing her green eyes.

Pete grinned. He already knew better than to give a customer the choice of spending less than a dollar. "You figure to capture the flag with this?" The crowd laughed as he handed over ten dimes.

The girl lifted one eyebrow and tossed a dime straight into one of the most expensive glasses.

"Best shot I've seen tonight." Pete wanted to add "honey" as Clarence did to any woman under fifty, but he couldn't seem to get it out.

The girl winked and tossed again. The dime fell to the canvas floor, and, still wondering what the wink might mean, Pete automatically reached down to scoop it up. He let out a yell as Clarence's bootheel came down sharply on his fingers.

"Didn't Carl warn you about picking up the change, Buster?"

Pete stared. Dimly he remembered Carl saying he and Clarence cleaned up the change that fell to the canvas floor.

"You don't have to stomp a guy for forgetting." Pete saw the girl scoop her remaining dimes and walk off. "You've chased off the customer."

"That so? Well, let me tell you, Bub, your *mistake* chased off that customer, and if it happens again you'll get worse than a stomping, you'll get fired. Ain't nobody's hand in *my* till." Clarence's beady eyes bored into Pete.

"I wasn't stealing. It's just natural to pick up something that falls—"

"Natural once more, and you're out. Remember that. Now back to work. I make allowance for your first night, or you'd be out now." Clarence turned to the crowd of customers watching bug-eyed.

Slowly Pete turned toward them, too. He forced himself to face people who thought he'd been stealing and willed himself to silence. However, when Clarence's back was turned, he quickly stuck out his tongue. A few of the marks laughed, and it made him feel a little better.

He felt a little better, but the last hour was a hard one. He wanted to cut out and tell Barney. *He'd* know whether they should tell Clarence off and clear out. Or maybe Carl would take his side? Not that he'd fire Clarence, he couldn't. But he could tell him to keep a civil tongue in his head. Barney would have a better idea if they *should* go to Carl.

Neither Clarence nor Pete had much to say as they closed the booth. Pete didn't know how to help, and Clarence didn't say. He just looked his way and scowled. Finally Pete sat down on a kitchen chair and waited. If Clarence didn't like him sitting, he could tell him what he wanted.

"OK, you're no help anyhow, might as well close up by myself. Go on—you're through—for tonight."

Pete held his breath during the pause. He thought Clarence was firing him and knew in that instance that he didn't *want* to leave. But it was only later, as he walked through the darkening midway toward the food wagon, that he wondered if Clarence had been going to fire him and changed his mind in that instant or if he were only taunting, trying to make him crawl. Well, he hadn't crawled and it would be a cold day in Hades before he did. Pete had coped with Clarences before.

The last customers were hanging around, finishing hot dogs and beers, prolonging the moment when they must leave the carnival. Pete thought some of the booths were pretty slow closing too, as if the carny people themselves preferred the lights and the music to the dark trailers.

A light breeze played along the runway, a relief after the hot still evening. It was quiet in the wake of the closing rides, and even the voices were muted so that Pete heard insects in the fields around them, and he felt his own anger drain. After all, he'd met worse guys than Clarence before.

The food wagon was dark. Barney had *said* he'd wait for him. He must be around somewhere. Then Pete noticed a dim light around the side of the wagon. He heard muffled voices, Barney's and a couple of others. Something told him to hesitate, to stand in the dark and listen a moment before barging in.

"Come on, sidecar, just a little seven will do it," he heard Barney call.

"Snake eyes. Tough luck."

"All right, let's get the show on the road. Show us, dude, show us. Ten. More like it. Let's have another ten."

Everyone seemed to be talking at once, and Pete couldn't tell from the voices who was winning except that after one explosion of laughter he heard Barney say he couldn't win them all.

He could see them now by the light of the two flashlights they had laid on the ground. It looked like a football huddle. They stood hunched over, the boy who threw the dice squatting a moment and then returning to the circle. The other crapshooters must be working in the floss wagon, too. The huddle broke apart, and there was Barney. In the flashlight's shadow, his eager face took on a queer alive intensity. And yet there was a distortion in the half-light, as if Pete were seeing a face in a funhouse mirror, so that joy and terror blended.

"Five bucks riding on this throw," Barney called.

There was a flurry of money and rolled dice. Again and again and a third time the dice raised dust so Pete wondered how they knew who won. Then Barney's face fell. He shrugged and raised one eyebrow. There was no doubt he'd lost five dollars, half a day's pay, on that roll.

Pete edged back to the path leading through the field toward the trailers. They'd only set up, and already the path was beaten down, the drying grass crackling underfoot. Maybe he should have said something, told Barney he was going on to bed? Maybe Barney would go by the dime toss and expect him to be waiting but, remembering the total absorption on Barney's face, Pete doubted that. Barney wouldn't remember they were to meet. It wouldn't cross his mind. Nothing would.

He pulled his sleeping bag from a truck cab and spread it on the flatbed of the big truck. Around him he could sense other roughies sleeping, and it gave him a good feeling. Which he needed. Both he and Barney had troubles this first night in the carnival. Pete crawled into his bag and lay looking at the stars a long while before he slept that night, but he did not hear Barney return.

Ten

A week later, on Sunday night, Pete leaned over the counter of the dime-pitch booth for a breath of fresh air. Almost midnight. It had been a hectic night, marks jamming the counter, throwing money at him—the boys showing off for the girls—the girls tight-lipped and throwing as if their lives depended on it. Everyone was smelling of hot dogs, popcorn, gum, and cheap perfume. All of it mixed with perspiration, and with cigarettes and alcohol. Nothing on earth smelled worse than someone else's beer. If only he could sleep an hour or two, he'd be able to snap back. But they were due to slough, to dismantle the carnival and head for San Antonio, the minute they closed. There would be no chance of sleep until dawn probably. He'd never make it, Pete thought dismally.

It was that moment when the crowd seemed to stop moving for a moment, when a hush fell over the lot. It came every night. Barney called it the "stop the world, I want to get off" time of night.

Barney. He was full of bitter capsule sayings these days. He was wound up so tight almost anything made him snap. He didn't like working in the food wagon. The smell of the cotton candy and hot dogs made him sick. But then, the whole carnival seemed to make him sick. Uneasy, he said. Pete thought that losing forty dollars in one week would make *him* uneasy, too. Barney would roll those dice twenty-four hours a day if he could. Said he came by it naturally, that these were his father's own dice. Maybe, but Pete thought someone should flush them down the toilet.

Well, Barney said he was cured—besides, he wasn't Pete's problem. They were just two guys who'd met on a beach and set off together across country. Once they reached Florida, they'd probably never see each other again. Those were the facts, but Pete knew they weren't the whole truth. The truth was that Barney was more like a brother than *any* of the foster brothers he'd had, and he was worried about him.

Pete was grateful when he heard the merry-go-round music slow down. The last ride. Must be closing early because of the teardown. All over the midway, rides were slowing down, jointees counting change, lights flashing and dimming. You could feel it in the customers' sleepy sadness, too. They hated to go home. Even after most of the lights were off, they still stayed around.

"Time to get on your horse, Pete," Clarence said, digging down into the deep pockets of his apron and bringing out handfuls of change and bills.

"Lots of folding money tonight," Pete noticed.

"Always is, the last night, marks know it's their last

90

chance. Want some coffee?" Clarence poured him a cup from his thermos without waiting for an answer. He added brown sugar and powdered cream and handed the concoction to Pete.

Pete gulped down the coffee. It would help keep him awake. Automatically he started putting the glasses back in cartons, then rolled down the canvas awning on all four sides of the booth so Clarence could scrounge for change on the floor and then count the take.

"How much?" Pete asked after the tally was done.

"Wouldn't you like to know, Bub? Yes, siree, wouldn't you just like to know? But one thing I will say, tonight's the best since you've been in the booth. Matter of fact, best of the season, so far. Better get it over to lock up before someone gets greedy," Clarence added, beaming. He carefully wiped his boots with a chamois cloth and adjusted his cowboy hat so that it tipped precariously over his right eye. He tucked in his shirt, snapped his wide red-and-white striped suspenders, and drew a deep breath. Then, taking a silver-tipped cane he used only when he deposited money in one hand and the heavy blue money pouch in the other, he stepped from the booth.

Pete wondered, as he had last Saturday when he was a greenhorn, if the cane contained a switchblade of some sort. Why else would Clarence tote it off to the office wagon? Unless it went with his closing-night dignity. Funny guy. It didn't make sense for him not to tell Pete what he made, especially since seventy-five percent went to Carl, and Carl would tell if he asked. However, it apparently made Clarence feel important, and he was one of those guys for whom this was everything. That had turned out to be what he was trying to prove that first night.

So, OK, the carnival was his life. Pete could live with that. He sighed and went on with the pack-up. He couldn't help slough with his bad shoulder, but he wanted to watch the men tearing down the carnival, so he hoped Clarence would make it snappy.

Half an hour later, he knew that both Clarence and Barney were overdue. He couldn't leave the booth until Clarence got back, and he could hear them dismantling the booths all around them. What he wanted to watch was taking down the Ferris wheel and the Mad Mouse. Where on earth *was* Clarence?

"Hey, Pete, open up." Barney was slapping the canvas, and Pete rolled it up enough for him to get in. Barney was flushed and excited.

"That Clarence—I've been waiting an age for him to come back and relieve me. I could help clean up the food wagon after the Ferris wheel comes down if you—"

"He'll be a while. There was an attempted holdup at the office wagon. They would have made it, too, if it hadn't been for that motorcycle gang that's been hanging around. About two dozen of those guys just surrounded the holdup men, guns and all—two men there were—and they started swinging their chains and switching open their knives. 'You can only get a couple of us, three at the most,' the head cyclist told the holdup men, 'and then we'll kill you both. You can take my word for that. Your other choice is to hand me the dough and leave. No more said. No word to the cops.' Well, I guess they thought it over a minute, handed over the dough, the motorcycle guys formed a passageway, and they left. Nobody else said a word, not one word."

"Then what did the motorcycle chief do with the

dough—?" Pete asked breathlessly, watching Barney work the dice in his left hand. There was such an excitement, a frenzy, to Barney's face that Pete could only burst out, "You were so lucky to be there!"

"Lucky? I could have been killed," Barney said in a hurt voice. "We *all* could have been killed. But, OK, just as cool as a cucumber the motorcycle guy went on back up to the cashier and said, 'Here, you take better care of this next time.' How's that for cool? And the owner and his family all making over them like they were kings. The cashier's probably still crying.

"Your pal, Clarence, was hopping around like a chicken with his head cut off, banging his cane all over the place, most likely trying to put out an eye. He's never had so much fun in all his born days. Just don't expect that one back for a while. Whew, let me sit down a minute. Such a lo-ong night. I kept getting seasick just watching that Ferris wheel throw cartwheels. And when a customer upchucks—and they do—it's all I can do to keep from joining in."

"But why would the motorcycle gang stick up for the carnival? They could have gotten themselves killed."

"Lots of the men here used to ride with cycle gangs. You should hear the tales they tell in the floss wagon. Better than the late late movies," Barney said casually.

"That's the good thing about your job. You have a chance to talk with the carny people. And all I get are the marks. If I—"

"In the food wagon we work about ten times as hard as anyone else, so don't complain. All I want to do is make back my losses and clear out. I talked with Lily tonight. She says you should come stay with us for a while."

Pete nodded. He didn't like to think about leaving the carnival. What was Barney's hurry? "You still thinking of going back to see Larsen?" he asked.

"Not much chance, the rate I'm losing. Listen, Pete, I'd like to stay and console you, but I hear teardown noises all over the lot, and my boss will boil me in oil if I don't clean the grease and cotton candy off the floor and walls. Lucky you, all you have to do is wait for old chatterbox, Clarence." Barney was suddenly restless.

"I'd trade."

Barney shrugged and was gone. "Meet you at the pickup," he called back.

Pete lifted the awning enough to watch Barney shuffle listlessly out into the hot night, already down again after the excitement of the holdup. Barney was *not* turned-on by cleaning the food wagon. That was obvious. And yet, he wanted to leave, to get back to it.

Pete envied him. If it weren't for his miserable arm, he'd prefer to work in the floss wagon where everyone in the carnival came for a hot dog or a cup of coffee.

Pete rolled up one canvas siding and looked out at the jointees taking down the other booths, calling back and forth in the still Texas night, teasing the girls from the girlie shows who hurried by, the bright feathers still in their high hairdos. He sniffed and caught the smell of midway sawdust and axle grease, good smells.

By the time he got out of the booth, the Ferris wheel and the Mouse would be dismantled. This was like seeing a ball game through a peephole. He yearned to be out there loading the trucks, which just showed how far gone he was when you considered the bad arm. They needed him like a hole in the head. Still, he could watch and learn

94

for when he *could* help.

He could see Clarence holding a postmortem on the holdup, going over every detail, forgetting they'd end up in the very last place in the caravan of more than fifty trucks Carl said the carnival formed in going from town to town. Waving his cane, imitating the cycle chief for everyone who hadn't been lucky enough to see for themselves. And then, when he'd exhausted that audience, knowing perfectly well he had a final captive audience in Pete, he'd probably talk all the way to San Antonio.

Pete had already been yearning to be part of the action, but suddenly he felt an added fury that Barney and Clarence should have seen the robbery, should have some part in the slough, while he stood looking out from the dime-pitch window, as usual. He reached up his arms and grabbed a two-by-four and shook the booth. He could probably even shake it apart. Then he wanted to run, run out into the night, across fields and along the hard macadam highway. He hadn't been for a good run in weeks. He could feel it in the soles of his feet, that highway. And then, out of the corner of his eye, unwillingly, he saw Clarence round the turn and come up the midway toward him, swinging his cane as Pete knew he would.

Then strangely, since he hadn't even thought of the Virgin Islands in days, he saw the beach and heard the palm trees and wondered if his aunt would be glad to see him.

Eleven

As the carnival vagabonded across Texas, from El Paso to San Antonio and on to Austin, it seemed to Pete that they wove a cocoon, becoming closer among themselves and more and more apart from the towns they played. And he was becoming a part of the carnival, considered a regular—Carl's boy—different from the casual labor they picked up to play individual towns. His arm was better, too, so that he could go in and help Barney clean up the floss wagon and meet everyone. He knew none of this impressed Barney and that he still looked forward to the time when they would leave the carnival and finish their trip. Pete also knew this had to come in another couple of weeks if he were going to reach the Virgin Islands in time to get a job and make arrangements for school, but he was beginning to wonder whether he wanted to leave at all. He was coming to feel curiously at home, comfortable in a way he could not remember feeling ever before.

There was something unreal about it all, too, as there was about Texas, as if the land itself were against decisions of any kind. He would sit on the edge of the fairgrounds where the flat brush prairie took over and stretched in three directions as far as he could see. The fourth side was always a city, also sprawling to the horizon. He'd never seen country on so grand a scale, where you saw the form of the land and the sky because there were no trees or houses to break the lines. And then he'd remember the Indians who used to come riding over this country, blending better than the automobiles that flowed like ants along raw-cut highways. Or he would pick up a handful of sand and watch the multicolored grindings sift through his fingers, sparkling in the hot sun. And the sun put a heat haze between him and the too-blue sky, between him and this land, so that the place itself pulled him back into the carnival community. At night he would have an old nightmare, one he used to dream when he was near the sea, and he couldn't understand why he was repeating it there, practically in the middle of a desert. He was swimming off a beach by San Francisco, China Beach, when he got tangled in seaweed. The more he fought, the tighter he was bound. He kept drifting out to sea in this seaweed shoal. He knew that he was entangling himself and that he *could* get out if he would only stop fighting, but he kept slashing away in his panic, the seaweed choking him, still telling himself he'd be all right if he could only relax. At this point he always woke up, drenched in sweat, flaying his arms in a last effort to fight off the sea gulls.

The sea gulls these days usually turned out to be Barney, trying to wake him, or one of the other roughies who shared the flatbed truck with them, telling him to shut up. Before—he did not like to say back home—he could always turn on a light and read himself back to sleep. If he turned on so much as a flashlight where he was, he'd be banished under the truck with the snakes and spiders. So he would lie back, trying to name all the constellations in the clear Texas sky until he fell asleep or found the morning star.

One night he lay there listening to the others' even breathing when Barney rolled over toward him.

"Hey, Pete, still awake?"

"Sure."

"I been wanting to ask you, what's this aunt of yours like, the one in the islands?"

"What brought *that* on?" Pete whispered.

"Oh, I been thinking—you ever meet her, for example?"

"That's what I'm planning to do in the Virgin Islands." Pete tried to carry it off lightly but his voice shook.

"But isn't that taking an awful chance? I mean Lily doesn't even want to see most of our relatives because they're either dull or want to borrow money, she says."

"I'm *not* depending on her, you know. I mean, she asked me. Go back to sleep before you wake the others. We can talk in the morning." Pete wondered if Barney thought his aunt had something to do with the bad dreams. Forget it.

The next day was their first in Austin, where the carnival played the county fair, the "pinnacle of profit and security," according to Clarence. It was during this ten-day stint that many of the concessions made a good part of their profit for the season, providing the weather and the crowds held. They also paid a higher rent for their space so there *was* some risk involved.

That afternoon Barney and Pete were sitting in the dime-pitch booth waiting for the carnival to open and listening to Carl and Clarence bickering about the pros and cons of playing county fairs.

"Just give me a mark with larceny in his heart— and I ain't never seen one without—and I'll make my stake on the Texas county fair circuit," Clarence said, slapping his knee.

"Only trouble is we pay so much for the privilege," Carl muttered, shaking his head. "And the worry is enough to make me break out in hives."

"Me, I'm looking for a certain *carny* with larceny in his heart," put in a young freckle-faced blond with a pack on his back. He leaned over the counter toward them.

"Take your choice," Carl advised the stranger with a sweep of his arm indicating himself, Clarence, Pete, and Barney. The newcomer smiled, a tight mirthless stretching of his lips that surprised Pete because he couldn't be much older than Barney and himself. He was tall and thin, and he wore Levi's and a white dress shirt, surprising again for someone carrying a pack on his back. His face looked tough, as if he might be in a motorcycle gang, except that he didn't dress like it.

"No, the man I'm tracking has a cast in his right eye, and he must be late thirties. Usually hires on as a mechanic. Wife and two kids in California." The boy shifted his pack.

"They sending alimony hunters out with packs on their

backs, these days?" Carl asked, snapping the cap of a Coke bottle, but not handing it over. He just kept it in his hand.

"Not yet. No, this is a personal matter."

"Grudge, huh? Have a Coke and take a load off your feet," Carl suggested then, unfolding a Samsonite chair and reaching it out to the boy. Carl never let a stranger inside the booth.

"My name's Barney, and this is Pete, and Carl and Clarence run this booth," Barney explained.

"Glad to meet you," the stranger said without volunteering his name.

"Where you from, Canada?" Clarence asked.

"Vancouver. How'd you know?"

"Relax. I'm not curious. Just the accent."

Pete and Barney looked at each other and laughed. If there was one thing Clarence was, it was nosy. Pete could tell from a grin, quickly erased, that the stranger knew this, too.

"Looking for a job, are you?" Clarence went on probing.

"Not yet. I'm a carny, or at least I've been working the Ford line this year, four months now, but like I said I'm tracking this guy that borrowed money and then flew out on me back at Sacramento, California. I want to know *why* he welshed is the truth of the matter, if you want to know."

"Can't say I blame you none for that," Clarence encouraged the speaker.

"I keep going over it in my mind, and the funny part is that he seemed like the one honest guy on the lot. Only guy I would have trusted, and he took me for a sucker.

Well, he taught me, all right. I only loaned it in the first place because he said his kid had pneumonia and he needed to send his wife all he could lay hands on. And that was the truth. I found his house and talked to his wife, and he *did* send the dough."

"At least there's that," Carl said.

"Hey, would you mind stopping that? Makes me nervous," the newcomer said to Barney, who was rolling his dice.

Barney put the dice in his pocket. After a silence the boy continued.

"The thing I want to know is why he run out when he pretended to be my friend. Been on his trail three weeks and don't figure to quit until I get the answer."

"Why'd you leave Canada?" Barney asked.

"Came down to join the Marines, and I'm waiting on my papers if you really want to know. They won't take me until I'm eighteen," he added reluctantly. "Could join Canadian service, but I don't want that."

"Was it a lot of money?" Clarence asked eagerly.

"Fact of the matter is, I got all but five dollars back. I attached his pay is how, after he left. I guess he didn't figure I'd go in to the cashier."

"You mean to sit there and tell me you've been tracking a man three weeks across three states because he owes you five dollars?" Barney asked, standing up out of his chair.

"It's the principle of the matter, you know. He *thought* he was gypping me of more. You don't welsh on a friend."

"You don't sound like much of a friend to me, attaching his pay and tracking him down like an animal. And what do you plan to do when you find the poor man?"

Barney went on, facing the stranger now, towering over the surprised boy.

"Hey, keep your shirt on, friend. What I do depends entirely on what he says, what account the man gives of himself."

"And suppose he just tells you to go fly a kite?"

"Hey, Barney, take it easy. This has nothing to do with you." Pete took Barney's arm, but he shook him off.

"No, I want to know. It's so stupid, tracking a man like an animal over five dollars. Here, I'll give you five dollars." And Barney pulled a crumpled five-dollar bill out of his pocket.

"Take it easy, Barney. This has nothing to do with you," Carl repeated quietly.

The boy shook his head. He was looking at Barney curiously. There was a mutual dislike. "Might be this, or the like, does have something to do with you, friend? It's not the lack of a five-dollar bill, at any rate. I've spent far more on this matter already. It's the principle of the matter. I want to know *why* he welshed on me, don't you see? Never could stand a welsher, could you?" He was eyeing Barney narrowly.

"There's worse things, like grudges," Barney said in a whisper, sitting down and staring at his hands.

The boy finished his Coke in the silence, stood up, and shouldered his pack.

"You haven't seen a man with a cast in his eye?"

Clarence shook his head and spoke with unusual kindness, "No, not in this show. We're mostly regulars here. You want my advice though, forget it. He's not worth your trouble."

"That's for me to say, friend. Thanks for the Coke."

He walked off without a backward glance.

Barney hadn't looked up, but after the boy was gone, Barney took out his worry dice and rolled them in his hand.

"All the way from Sacramento, California, over five lousy dollars. That guy has to be one of the real crazies of all time," he said slowly. "I'd hate to think someone would track one of us down over five dollars."

"Nope, he's not crazy, just a carny. That's the way some of them think. Honor among thieves, I guess," Carl said with an embarrassed laugh. "Not all of us would go traipsing after five dollars. Not me, for example. But I've known others. That's why I keep telling you boys to give it up and go back to school—"

Barney stood up and, without a word, left the booth at a run.

"Hey, Barney, wait up," Pete called, starting up the midway after him. But Barney had ducked around a corner, and Pete couldn't see anything but the heat rising from asphalt, shimmering like a clammy morass between him and Barney. As he ducked back into the booth, the smell of Coca-Cola and Clarence's pipe tobacco hit him like the memory of another afternoon, one also dominated by tobacco (Bull Durham) and the too-sweet residue of Coca-Cola.

He was trying to remember what afternoon that was, sorting the ragbag of his memory for this combination of heat and smells so that he could supply the geographic picture and the time, but he could not. He was surprised to realize Carl had been talking and was now expecting some answer. He tried to switch his mind to recapture the sounds and sort *them* out, but he gave that up and, shrugging, asked:

"Come again, Carl?"

"I said, do you want me to ask around and find out whether Barney's rolled up some heavy bets?"

Pete shook his head. "No thanks. Barney just didn't like the guy's attitude, that's all."

"Looked to me like Barney had a guilty conscience," Clarence said.

Twelve

"Oh, why doesn't he give the signal to pull over?" Carl asked. "We'll be awash or over the side in five minutes if this keeps up."

They were on the road again; Pete, Barney, and Carl sharing the cab of the pickup truck, on their way to Houston. Carl had mentioned an hour before that the flies swarming around the long line of carnival trucks were a sure sign of rain. The sky had been blue, but soon after it had darkened with racing clouds, and now the storm had broken. Lightning rolled into thunder again and again until the sky seemed to Pete to be exploding like a battlefield. The drops gathered and soon the rain was a torrent, pelting the line of fifty-six trucks, pushing and blinding them dangerously on the raised highway.

"I can't see a thing through the windshield," Barney whispered, freckles standing out on his frightened face. "We could roll if we go over the edge. Sure glad it's not me driving."

"You're a comfort," Carl answered tightly. "Why doesn't that fool flash the pull-over signal?"

"Maybe there's no place *to* pull over," Pete suggested.

They drove in silence after that for a few minutes, hearing only the rain. Thunder and lightning had stopped momentarily. Pete could see only the taillights from the truck ahead and the red tip of Carl's cigarette. The storm was like a gray night.

" 'Bout time," Carl said as the left-turn signal flashed ahead.

Gradually the trucks slowed. The brake lights flashed on ahead of them. Lightning tore at the sky, and Pete wondered what it was you did if the truck were hit. Didn't metal attract lightning? Could you survive if you didn't touch any metal part of the truck or anyone who touched metal?

The line of trucks had pulled out of the traffic and over to the side of the highway. Pete heard screeching brakes and braced himself for the dull crunch of colliding cars, the skidding, a slipping like the feeling of falling out of bed just before you get to sleep. If only they didn't flip over—

"Put away those *dice* before I shove them down your throat."

"Sorry," Barney said, slipping them in his pocket. "I know now I couldn't be a truck driver. I don't have the guts," he whispered.

"Well, you don't have to sound so relieved."

"I am relieved, Carl. My dad drove a semi for twenty years, almost."

Carl nodded but kept looking at the wall of water cascading down the windshield, inching his way behind squealing brakes, pulling gingerly to a stop himself.

"Made it again," he said as he took his hands tentatively off the wheel, stretching his fingers wide, pulling and cracking each knuckle. Then Carl wiped the sweat off his forehead and down into his beard, patting his neck dry. He'd been chewing at his underlip before, and Pete watched him lick the lip, taste blood, shrug, and daub the spot with the sweaty handkerchief. Then he laid his head back and closed his eyes.

The rain still drummed the truck but they were safe and warm and dry, while outside on the great highway other cars flashed by, brakes and horns screaming under the pressure of the storm. *They* were out of it.

Carl seemed to be asleep. His mouth fell open. Pete turned to Barney, started to speak, and waited. There was an expression of peace, almost bliss, on Barney's face. As if he'd taken an overdose of tranquilizers.

"You were really worried?"

"About what?" Barney looked surprised.

"Cracking up, turning over, getting struck by lightning—"

Barney laughed happily. "Forget *that!* I guess we *have* stopped, but I hadn't noticed." Barney looked curiously out into the sheets of rain and then over at Carl, who opened one eye.

"That cackling of yours woke me up."

"Sorry, Carl, I was feeling good because I'm never going to have to be a truck driver, no matter what!"

"Get another hang-up, Barney. That one's getting old. Freedom. Liberation. No one has to follow in his father's footsteps. Do your own thing—providing you can think something up. But just leave me out of it. Why do you

107

think I didn't have kids of my own? So I can sleep, is why." Carl closed his eyes again.

A few minutes later, Carl sat up and leaned over the wheel. "Well, *say* something. I can't sleep with all that breathing going on. Sounds like a couple of walruses in the cab. You don't want to drive trucks, Barney, don't. But there's worse ways to make a living."

"Lily says my dad always followed the path of least resistance and I slopped out of the same bucket and she did too. It runs in our family. But I've always been afraid of cars, ever since I can remember, and now I just know that's one thing I *won't* do, drive a truck. I *don't* have to. Does that make any sense at all, Carl?"

"Good sense." The big man leaned over and smiled, nodding. Pete winced. He felt as if some secret were passing between the two. He wanted to say something but checked himself. He wasn't going to go pushing in where he wasn't wanted. That's what he'd promised himself back on that beach the night he'd run away, and it still held. Another couple of weeks at the most and he'd never see either of these guys again, so what did it matter if they didn't ask his opinion? Pete was tempted to open the truck door and walk away over the prairie. Do your worst, storm, he could see himself saying, shaking his fist at the sky. Instead he turned against the window and pretended he was asleep. The rain pelted the window so that it beat against his cheek. And the pain had come back in his arm.

The next day, the city of Houston was clearing up after the storm. After they'd set up their booths, Pete and Barney were free for the afternoon.

Pete wondered later what made him decide to go to the

zoo with Barney that particular afternoon. It had been Barney's suggestion, though Pete had never heard him mention animals one way or the other before. There'd been a time when Pete had been a zoo nut, particularly a lion lover, but after he'd seen on television how much healthier lions and other animals photographed in the wild looked, he'd given up going to zoos. He wondered what made Barney want to go.

Maybe just because this had been a day to go somewhere. Brilliant and newly washed clean, Houston seemed full of excitement. Pete felt he could walk forever, breathing in the drying, steaming city. Even the torrid heat had broken after the storm, and people had an alertness about them, as if they too were grateful for the unusual respite at the end of July.

Barney was quiet on the bus. Unusual but welcome. Pete could get a look at the city, the wide lawns rolling back to big white houses, shuttered against the sun. There were a lot of dogs, and he liked that.

Mostly, he was glad to have a day off. The dime pitch was getting to be a drag, night after night. All the customers were beginning to look alike, big hands with dirty fingernails nervously cracking knuckles before throwing to hit the sixteen-ounce glass or the cookie jar. And Clarence! If Pete *never* saw that miser scuffing the canvas floor with his pointy-toe boots again, gleaning every single dime, it would be too soon.

"There better not be many like Clarence in the Virgin Islands," he said, startled to hear his own voice. Talking to himself was getting to be a bad habit.

"Your aunt is probably a dead ringer for Clarence," Barney answered. "Most likely she'll charge enough to make a profit on your room and board."

"I have no intention of living with Aunt Lenore, and I may not even look her up, so lay off! How come you're so down on someone you've never even met, anyhow?"

"Think you're riding for a fall, that's all," Barney muttered, looking out the window.

"That's my problem then, OK?"

"I think you'd be better off with us. Suppose it all blows up with your aunt—what happens to school?"

"I didn't know school meant so much to you." Pete intended a voice dripping with sarcasm, but he only managed to sound astonished. "Look I've had homes blow up on me before, and I always kept up my grades. They're my scholarship to college, and I know that. *Come on, Barney*—"

Barney shrugged, and neither of them spoke again until they entered the zoo and sat down on a sunny bench across the moat from two brown bears. As soon as they sat down, one bear ambled over to the edge and proffered a paw. Pete and Barney looked at each other and laughed.

"Just like Clarence," Pete said, throwing a peanut.

"Sure, they're both starving. After all, Carl makes the profit," Barney said with a touch of bitterness, tossing out another peanut. The bear caught Pete's and then searched around until he found the other nut and scooped that up too before returning to his mate.

"Pete—how soon do you figure to leave—the carnival, I mean?"

"Pretty soon, I guess. Why?" Pete felt a sinking in his stomach. It was the question he'd been asking himself the last several days and put off answering.

"Well—I been trying to decide whether to wait for you.

I want to blow. First there was the holdup and then that nut tracking down his buddy, and all we ever *do* is work. I hope I never see cotton candy again if I live to be a hundred. Lily's in Florida, and she's waiting for us. But—"

"Hold on. You don't need an alibi. I'm ready. There's plenty of guys here want our jobs, so that's no sweat. We can catch a bus out the minute Carl gets someone to take our shifts." Pete threw more peanuts to the bears and gave them full attention for a few minutes.

"Makes you blue though, doesn't it?"

"Had to come. Yeah, I like this life, but they'll be sticking in Texas another month, almost. I should be in the islands now, really."

Barney grinned, relieved. "Carl probably won't even miss us. Lily's at this fabulous trailer court—swimming pool, recreation room—"

"Lily. Lily. How do you know where she is all the time to make those phone calls? Sounds like you got constant contact."

Barney pulled a rumpled sheet of paper from his shirt pocket. "Lily used to be a travel agent. So she made me out an itinerary—where she'd be and when she'd be with friends so I could call her. See, even in Miami."

Pete fingered the paper curiously. It looked like Barney had worn it out. Something about it made him mad, as if it took the edge off Barney's adventure and even his own. He wanted to say something cutting about being a mama's boy, but he was too aware of how hard it must have been for a person like Lily to keep to an itinerary. She must have hated *having* to be at so and so's by 7 P.M.

"Did she give it to you before we left?"

"No, mailed it to El Paso, care of the carnival."

Pete nodded, trying to take it all in.

"There were only four places I could get in touch," Barney said defensively, as if he knew what was going through Pete's mind.

"Oh, I was thinking about your grandmother's being a travel agent," Pete lied.

Barney accepted that. "Pete, there's just one thing. I been thinking of hitching—" Barney looked down at his hands.

"I'd rather take the bus."

"Right."

Barney sat working his dice. The bear across the moat reared on his hind legs and both boys automatically threw him peanuts. Pete laughed and looked over to Barney, but Barney wouldn't meet his eyes. He looked sick.

"I can't take the bus," he said finally, mumbling the words.

"How much do you owe?" Pete asked with a hard edge to his voice.

Barney looked up and then down at the dice in his hands. "If I get out of this, I will never so much as bet on the time of day. Tell me the truth, Pete, am I the worst fool that ever lived?"

"*Stop* feeling sorry for yourself! Don't be such a baby. *How much,* Barney?"

"Within five bucks of everything I got, including pay owed me. I would have been ahead if I'd quit a week ago. If I stay much longer, I'll wind up in debt the rest of my life. I know that much."

"Put those dice away, then, and let me think." The only thing he *could* do was pay Barney's way to Florida, though it would probably take a week's wages. He couldn't leave Barney to get further in debt. It would serve him right but—

"I been thinking I could borrow from Carl, but I hated to ask an outsider—"

Pete looked up quickly. "No, no, let's keep it between ourselves," he said gently, with a curious rush of pride. "I can handle it." And then, suddenly rough, "And give me those *dice* and let's get moving."

"I know Lily will pay you back when we get to Miami."

Pete grabbed the dice out of Barney's hand and started to leave. Across the path, he turned. "Come *on,* Barney!"

Thirteen

Carl had driven them downtown to the main Greyhound Bus station, and now the three of them stood on the black-and-white checkered floor, like pawns on a chessboard waiting to be moved, waiting for the express to Miami. Pete fingered his ticket. He noticed the other people standing on their squares, also marking time, mostly alone. At least they didn't have to worry because they couldn't think of anything to say. He looked up at the wall clock and caught Carl watching it, too, possibly worrying about his booths at the carnival. He *should* leave. It was only nine, and it would be another ten minutes before they could hope to get on the bus. Somehow, Pete could not tell Carl to go ahead and leave. He *should,* though, because Carl would be needed to break in their replacements.

Barney looked miserable, just as he had when it was time to say good-bye the morning he and Pete had first met on the beach—only a little more than a month ago. In a few more days it would be good-bye for them, too.

"I know I'm forgetting something important," Barney said.

Carl smiled. "You'll be glad to get home." It wasn't a question.

"I miss Lily and my own bed—but I'll miss you, too."

"You can't win them all." Carl laid his hand briefly on Barney's shoulder. "Tell Lily I'm expecting dinner when I hit Miami."

"Come home and stay with us," Barney invited.

"Home? You've never even *been* to Miami, have you?" Pete asked, and he was surprised at how indignant his voice sounded.

"The trailer's been my home ever since I can remember," Barney said quietly.

"Oh, sure." Pete felt his face flush.

"Way I heard it, you're invited to that dinner, too, but you prefer the Virgin Islands to the likes of us, right Pete?" Carl asked, looking straight into Pete's eyes.

"I don't prefer *anyone* to you guys. It's just something I have to do." Pete looked right back at Carl. Then they both smiled.

"Can't argue with a man's dream."

Pete let that go, and they were silent again. People pushed around them. They were supposed to be in line for door number two, but the lines had become one solid jam of bodies, baggage, and lost children. Everyone seemed to have lost whatever sense of direction they'd had coming in. Not that Pete was putting them down for that. The main reason he and Barney were so glad to get an express bus was that then they couldn't get the wrong bus in some little town and wind up in New York instead of Miami.

"I *still* think you should have taken a local and seen something of the country. When will you ever get a chance to be in Mississippi or Alabama again? Where's your sense of adventure?" Carl's voice was ironic, as if he knew why they were taking the express.

"That's" why we joined the carnival," said Barney in the same tone of voice.

"I'll write you about my sense of adventure from the Virgin Islands." Pete grinned. And then he waited. Maybe Carl didn't want to write. So far as Pete knew, Carl'd never written a letter all the time they'd been together.

"And I'll tell you about Miami and Lily," Barney added eagerly.

"That so? I never seen either of you lunkheads so much as make out a postcard, so I'll believe it when I see the whites of the envelopes. It's a nice thought, though, at that. Otherwise I might have to report back to Larsen that a barracuda swallowed Pete the very first day, off one of those reefs, and Barney got lost in the wilds of Disneyland."

"Tell the guru I'm going to send money and stuff for my horoscope first thing I *get* some money," Barney said, flushing.

"Better toss out those dice or *that* won't be soon." Carl crushed his cigarette with the toe of his boot.

Both boys waited to see if he would say anything more. Pete wondered how much Carl knew about Barney's gambling. Barney was looking down at the floor, as if he were expecting to be bawled out. Carl watched him for a moment, looked over at Pete, and shrugged.

"Wish I'd had half the sense of either of you when

I was your age. Now pick up your bags and get moving or all the old ladies in Houston will crowd in ahead of you."

The line was moving, and the boys went with it, looking back for a last glimpse of Carl just in time to see him push through the doors to the outside. He did not look back.

"He didn't even give us a chance to thank him," Barney said as they found seats and looked back into the lighted waiting room.

"We can write."

"Maybe. He didn't say we should come back and work for him again next year, though."

"Come on, Barney. Can you imagine Carl saying something so—so—like an employer?" They both laughed, but later, as the bus lurched through town after town in the night, Pete wondered why it should have seemed so ridiculous Carl might behave like other people. He just wouldn't have made an empty promise, or any promise, for that matter. Carl took everything as it came. He wasn't surprised when they climbed into his truck and rode across country, when they joined the carnival, or when they quit. Pete wished he'd asked Carl about himself but, of course, that would have been *absolutely* impossible.

He envied Barney, who had fallen asleep before they were out of Houston. Half the people on the bus seemed to be snoring. The other half were smoking or drinking. Beer, wine, and stale popcorn. Carnival smells. Clarence would have to do some work tonight, for a change. Pete smiled in the dark bus and then, restless, he pulled a book out of his pocket and snapped on the light over his head.

Fourteen

P̲ete was still groggy from thirty-six hours on the bus, so what happened seemed like a dream. At first.

The thing he couldn't believe was that they'd walked directly out of the Miami Greyhound Bus station and into the arms of the cops. At ten o'clock in the morning. They'd come out into the sunshine, asked a shoeshine man the way to the beach, and then felt this tap on the arm.

"Say, buddy, can we see your ID?" the first one asked. Blue uniform, star, everything.

"Have any cash?" The other cop, a guy who didn't look as if he'd been shaving very long himself, added.

Barney looked as if he were about to pass out. He was half-asleep from a day and a half on the bus and then this. He'd already stuck his hand into his pocket when Pete shook his head.

"No, but we're looking for a job, officer," Pete said. Everybody at the carnival said the police were out for a handout, and he didn't intend to lose his money. Too much depended on it. Besides, they might be suspicious of a kid like him carrying two hundred dollars in traveler's checks plus almost forty in cash. These guys must wait for everyone who came out of the bus station with a pack on his back.

"We don't have enough jobs for our own teenagers, son. Why don't you just go on back in and hop on another bus?" The older man spoke kindly, but he wasn't giving them a choice.

"But we haven't done anything," Barney whispered.

Pete had this crazy desire to laugh. He had to clamp his mouth shut.

"Just making sure you don't use us for a pad," the young cop said, and the word sounded like one he was cultivating.

"But we *live* here. I mean, we're going to. We're just on our way to phone my grandmother," Barney said, obviously relieved.

"Oh, she know you're in town?"

"Thought I heard you asking the shoeshine the way to the beach. That doesn't sound like telephoning grandma."

That was when Pete burst out laughing. He couldn't help it, getting hung because they wanted to see the beach before phoning was too much. The stricken look on Barney's face was too much. It was like a scene from *The Three Stooges*. He stood there laughing, and the cops were getting redder in their faces, and Barney looked ready to make a run for it.

"All right, wise guy, why don't we just phone grandma from the station house. All right? The car's parked right there on the corner."

So that was how they came to be sitting in this tight little room in the station with a varnished oak library table between them. Barney had relaxed a little after he found out they weren't being booked or fingerprinted, but he was staying clear of Pete, sitting head down, arms folded across his chest, waiting it out while the man phoned Lily.

"Come on, Barney, look at the bright side. This saves us the dime for a phone call."

Barney closed his eyes.

"Why the big fear? You haven't broken a single law— OK, sulk, baby—"

The real mystery, Pete decided, was why Barney gambled if he was such a rabbit about the law. He was sitting there with his hands clenched, scared to death, and by tomorrow he'd be rolling the dice again. And they *would* land him in the county jail eventually. Did he really play those dice because his father had and they were a big keepsake? That didn't make much sense, but not knowing a father himself, Pete couldn't say how he might have felt. The other strange thing about Barney was that he never mentioned his mother. He must have had one. Pete turned his head. The older policeman was back.

"All right, boys, you're clear. Barney, your grandmother says to tell you she'll be here in half an hour to take you out to the fanciest lunch in Miami," the cop said, smiling.

"How'd my grandmother take it?" Barney asked.

"Yeah, what did she say?" There was a threat still in the young cop's voice, and Pete suddenly remembered he was a runaway. It was the first time in days he'd thought about it or about California at all, for that matter. But it wouldn't be good if someone happened to run a routine check. It could be *very* bad. He *could* land back in California.

"She's a little put out—a *very* vocal lady, Sam—but she's mad at the Miami police, of course. Says neither boy has *ever* been in trouble," the big man said, nodding his head.

"Oh, brother, one of those. Think I'll take an early lunch."

Pete smiled. They weren't going to run any check if they thought Lily would raise a fuss.

The middle-aged policeman brought in an armload of old magazines, and the two men left. Barney gave Pete one dirty look before he buried himself in a sports article.

Pete shrugged. "Oh, come on, Barney. They didn't book us. What have you lost? After all, how would you ever have gotten to know what the inside of the Miami police station was like if I hadn't laughed?"

Barney said nothing and did not look up. Pete considered the possibility that he was so deeply involved in the article that he hadn't heard, but some tenseness in the way Barney sat, some tautness, said Barney had heard him loud and clear. He wondered what Barney would do if he let out a bloodcurdling scream, a real chiller.

"But it *was* funny," Pete insisted quietly. This was the first time Barney had ever been mad at *him,* and it was over the cops' mistake, not his. Anything he couldn't stand, it was a sulker. He'd known enough sulkers to last a lifetime, and he hadn't done one thing to this one. He reached over and tapped Barney's toe lightly with his own foot. Barney's head jerked up.

"Let me tell you one thing—two things. First, you are more likely to land in jail than I am at the rate you're going. And number two—when you are in a jam, you stick together with your buddies!" Pete's voice was furious, menacing. Barney's eyes widened, but he didn't look away. "If your grandmother pays me back your bus fare, I'll catch a flight out tomorrow, and you'll never have to be embarrassed by *my* crude behavior again but you may run into worse," Pete added bitterly, burying himself behind a magazine. Over the top he saw Barney flush crimson, start to speak, and change his mind. *That* should take care of him, Pete thought with satisfaction.

The silence between them was so complete that when they heard Lily it sounded like a platoon coming down the hall. Both boys looked up to see Lily standing in the doorway, followed by half the Miami police force. She stood there in a floppy hat, smiling, and there was something so pleased in her eyes when she caught sight of them, that Pete burst out:

"Lily! I've never been so glad to see anyone in my whole life." And then he remembered he'd really only seen her once before.

Barney looked sick, and for a moment he didn't say anything. Then he wiped one hand across his eyes and burst out, "But you're—in a dress! I mean, you look nice." Barney blushed as everyone laughed.

"You're supposed to pretend this is the normal me— and you, let's have a look at *you*," Lily cried, throwing her arms around Barney and giving Pete a wink over her shoulder.

The same kind of wink that Barney gave if something amused him, Pete thought grudgingly. He knew what

Barney meant about the dress. It looked as if she'd borrowed it from some old lady. It was a yellow sack, and the stockings and black shoes must have come out of the same secondhand store. She wore no makeup, and her hair was severely tied back into a bun. She'd still rock most PTA meetings, but she'd obviously gone to some trouble to make herself look respectable enough to spring them from the law.

She held Barney off at arm's length and looked over at the police, who were grinning at her. "Well, gentlemen, a month on his own has done my grandson a world of good. He's filling out—going to be brawny like his father. But," she paused and eyed the police sharply, "I think it is a shame that law-abiding boys, good boys, can't get off a bus without facing false arrest. I can't be bothered suing you, but next time someone will. Men like you not taking a boy's word—shame on you." Lily wagged her finger at the men, and they fidgeted, looking embarrassed.

"Missus, nobody's been arrested, and if you'll just sign this, you're all free to go—" the middle-aged policeman said gently, wearily. "I've tried to explain—"

Lily took the clipboard and read it carefully. When she looked up, her eyes were snapping.

"This—document—says they're being *released* to my custody—as if the whole mess weren't *your* mistake from start to finish. Ri-dic-ulous!"

Pete watched as Lily wrote *"this does not apply to us"* across the paper and handed it back to the older policeman. They looked at each other a moment, and then the man shrugged. Lily turned to Pete and Barney, beckoned with her index finger, and left the room. The rest of the men silently moved aside. Pete and Barney got into their packs, and Pete strode out of the room, imitating Lily. He liked her style. *She* would have laughed along with him.

Barney stood, hesitating, looking after his grand-mother and Pete.

"Well, good-bye. I'm sorry," he said and, adjusting the pack, left too.

"So long," one of the men said.

The police station had been dark and air-conditioned, and the muggy noon heat hit them full tilt. It was a dense humid warmth that seemed to rise from the pavement in continuous steam jets. And the glare and smog stung at Pete's eyes. The noise—honking, braking, a loudspeaker advertising a skating rink, and the tinkle of an ice-cream vendor battered Pete as he stood at the top of the Miami police department steps, blinking into the sun. And over it all came the smell of fading roses. If anything, other than exhausts, this city should smell of the sea salt, but it did not. Roses.

Lily was the first to recover. "Well, your old grand-mother's good for something, even if it *is* only bailing you out. I did all right, didn't I?" Lily unbuttoned the first three buttons at the neck of her dress.

"You were great," Pete congratulated her.

"Pete *had* to laugh, or we wouldn't have been there in the first place," Barney said, still sullen.

"So you got to see the inside of the station. Lucky break." Lily laughed, turning to Pete. "And you're a sight for sore eyes, Pete. How's the arm?" She gave Pete a tentative hug, out of deference for the injury. It was obvious she couldn't remember which arm had been in-volved. Pete found himself hugging her back. The first time he'd ever hugged anyone. He let go quickly, but the memory of lavender and softness was strangely pleasant.

"Wow, you'll take the wind out of me, young man." Lily grinned, pleased. "And how is Carl and did you like carnival life and the country and—oh, you'll like the new trailer court, Barney, lots of trees and dogs and a recreation room with pool table and slot machines and—a swimming pool!"

"Great! About being picked up—"

"Don't apologize for their mistake!" Lily cut him short. "And don't blush. It allows people to take advantage of you," she added sharply, peering up at Barney, who towered above her. She was slightly stooped as well as short, which gave her an owlish expression as she cocked her head sideways and peered up at the boys from under the brim of her hat.

"That's a great hat," Pete said, admiring the fine soft weave.

"I bought it last week. Miami has a good Salvation Army, although I must say it's not the place to shop it once was. Too many hippies, who should be shopping at Macy's, are driving the prices up—but the point is, where do we eat? Sky's the limit. What do you want to celebrate —tacos, chicken, steak, spaghetti?"

"Lily always wants to celebrate," Barney said, and he smiled wistfully at Pete, who nodded.

"Then let's celebrate," Pete replied, sensing that Barney was finally ready to forget about his laughter. And now either Lily had some money and would pay him back and he'd be leaving or she didn't and he might wait around a few days.

They stood in the hot sun considering. Pete had never been to a "sky's the limit" restaurant. In fact he'd never been anywhere except a burger stand until Carl took them to the A-1 Truck Stop. He'd seen them in movies—the man and girl were all dressed up and the waiter bowed them clear across the room to a table for two with a rose on it.

"I—don't think I have the right clothes," Pete said.

"Chicken," Barney said. "I mean to eat."

"How about lobster?" Lily asked. "Clothes don't matter until after five."

"Oh."

"I think I know just the place. Chandeliers and white tablecloths, they said on TV. And air-conditioning," Lily added, taking off her hat and fanning her face.

Fifteen

"Sky's the limit," Lily said grandly as she pulled her old Buick into the almost-empty restaurant parking lot. Not more than a dozen cars stretched out in the vast paved area. Two Cadillac types and a few small foreign cars. Pete recognized a Mercedes. They all looked new, and they gleamed against the steaming white of the lot. The Buick must be a dozen years old and hadn't been washed at least since the trip from California. Its crumpled front fenders had long since rusted. Heavy-duty springs and the trailer hitch tilted up its rear end, and the side windows were plastered with decals from the various parks where Lily had spent a night or two over the years. Nevertheless, as Lily said, the attendants needn't have given the impression that there was barely room for the car.

Those attendants turned out to be polite compared to the waiters inside the Plaza restaurant. Pete had the feeling that only their unsuitable Levi's, plaid shirts, and long hair were visible to the waiter who led them to a table in the darkest corner of the room. He did not see their faces.

He waited for Lily to complain, since almost all the tables were empty, but she sat there as cowed as he and Barney. All three of them hid behind menus. Almost any meal cost as much as Barney and Pete had spent on food during the entire five-day trip to Texas with Carl. The waiter stood with his pencil poised, but between the prices and his dirty clothes Pete kept forgetting what he'd just read.

The waiter sighed.

"Sky's the limit," Lily repeated, but her voice sounded a little hollow. "Why not try lobster tails?" Lobster tails were the most expensive dinner on the menu, and Lily glanced up at the waiter.

The waiter sighed again.

It *would* show the waiter if he ordered those lobster tails, but Pete had never tasted them, and he hated to waste *this* meal. "Chicken," he said, and instantly *everything* else on the menu looked better. But the waiter was already writing down his order.

"Spaghetti! But that's what I *want*," Barney added defensively as Lily raised one eyebrow.

So Lily had to order the lobster tails for herself. Pete wanted the waiter to leave so he could get a real look at their surroundings.

"Roquefort, Thousand Island, or oil and vinegar?" the waiter asked, shifting feet.

"Chicken, spaghetti, and lobster tails," Lily murmured absently, sniffing at the single red rose in the center of their table.

"What kind of *salad dressing*, please, madam?"

They all had Thousand Island.

"Onion or tomato soup?"

"Tomato," they stated in exasperated unison.

"Wine?" This time Pete thought he heard a definite sneer. He'd given up hope the waiter would ever leave and simply waited to see what he'd ask next. He'd noticed that every time the waiter asked another question, his neck darted forward like a snake, his lips parted slightly.

"Coffee for me. Iced tea for both boys." Lily stared the waiter down, and he finally backed away.

"I suppose you might be able to get jobs as waiters, summers, if you got really hard up," she commented. "But just look at that velvet wallpaper. I'd give a pretty penny to have *that* in the trailer."

"You sure would. I wouldn't mind having the rug either," Barney muttered, still subdued.

It was a pleasure just to drink ice water from the stemmed goblet, Pete thought. He leaned back on the padded chair and gingerly fingered the starched napkin. The silverware and the tall silver salt-and-pepper shakers gleamed even though there were curtains over the windows so the restaurant light was dim. There must have been a hundred tables, and each one had its white tablecloth and real silver and the single red rose. The rug was so thick he had felt as if he was walking on sponge rubber, and the velvet wallpaper with its own cut roses *was* beautiful. In fact, this was the most beautiful room he'd ever seen in his whole life. He couldn't get over the feeling that he was watching a movie, that pretty soon the lights would go up and he'd have to leave.

"You know," Barney said, "some people probably eat here everyday."

"All it takes is money." Lily was waving away another waiter who darted out to the table every time anyone took a drink of water and hovered, waiting to fill the glasses.

"I've never been anywhere like this," Pete said shyly.

"Well, seemed like it was time for a celebration. You two being home from the carnival, full of adventures and all."

"Don't remind me," Barney groaned.

The waiter brought the soup, and Pete thought Barney made a pig of himself on the different kinds of crackers that came along, neatly arranged in a silver bowl.

"We'll let you know when we need water, son." Lily was getting control of the waiter. "Probably afraid he'll lose his job if he doesn't look busy, and there aren't many customers yet. Hovers like a hummingbird."

Lily pursed her lips when the waiter brought everyone Roquefort dressing.

"As long as it's only salad, it's good to try something new," she commented and handed him the cracker tray to refill.

She and Barney talked a little about high school and the trailer court, and Pete kept listening for some clue to their finances, to figure out if she'd be able to pay back his loan to Barney. It wouldn't be too bad to stay on for a while at a trailer court with a swimming pool. He *should* write his aunt he was coming first, anyhow.

By the time the waiter brought the entrées, Pete was filled up with soup and crackers and salad. Which was just as well as it turned out, because Pete saw he'd made a terrible mistake. Half a baked chicken lay in a nest of rice. In one piece. There didn't seem to be a good way to

130

get any meat off with a knife and fork. He certainly couldn't pick it up and start gnawing away. Not in the Plaza! Bravely, he picked up the knife and fork and began to eat what he could get, mainly skin.

"How is the chicken, Pete?" Lily asked. She hadn't yet touched her lobster.

"Oh, really great!"

"And the spaghetti, Barney?"

Pete looked over, and Barney was trying to spin spaghetti around his fork. He'd get it about halfway to his mouth, and the spaghetti would slither off the fork and return to the plate, like a gopher snake going back to its hole. Once he had his mouth open, and spaghetti slipped off and into his lap. He wadded it up in his napkin, blushing furiously, and set his fork down by his plate. In a few minutes he picked up the fork again but he was clearly just going through the motions.

"Try slipping your spoon under and lift it up that way," suggested Lily.

"Is it polite?"

"The president does it. I saw it once on television. But how on earth does anyone get the lobster *out* of his shell if you can't use your fingers?" Lily asked, looking straight at Pete.

"Don't ask me. I only know about them live." He laughed, and pointed to his uneaten chicken. No one had ordered anything he could respectably eat.

"Country bumpkins, starving to death in the best restaurant in Miami," Lily said, and they all burst out laughing.

"Waiter, hey waiter, how about bringing us some doggie bags. Pronto!" Lily turned to the boys. "We've seen

131

the best restaurant in town, and it looks like we've gotten a good meal, but now we're going to go home and enjoy it."

"And next time, I'll order steak," Barney said as they stood in the brilliant sunlight outside the restaurant.

"Someday, Lily, I'm going to buy you wallpaper just like that in the restaurant—for your trailer," Pete said quietly.

"Well, that's a dandy offer—if you'll put it on the walls once it comes. And speaking of walls, there's a nice little trailer for sale, heard about it from a friend, that might be just about right for a room for the two of you—we could park it in the spot I've already got—oh, I asked the manager—"

"But, Lily, you know—"

"Sure, sure, the Virgin Islands. Don't say anything now, Pete. Think it over carefully for twenty-four hours before you say one word. I mean that. You could stay on here a couple of years, get high school under your belt, and *then* go on down to the islands. Hush now, I don't want to hear one word until—" Lily looked at her watch. "Until 1:37 tomorrow afternoon. I mean that."

Pete shook his head. It was too much. He felt stifled. The humidity must be what made it so hard to breathe. He looked at Lily, and she smiled back happily. Barney smiled too. Pete felt ambushed. His stomach turned over queasily. What he'd like, what he'd *really* like to do, would be to turn and walk away, but Lily would probably come after him with a flying tackle. He got into the car with the definite feeling that the next twenty-four hours were going to be pure hell.

Sixteen

No more had been said about staying, but Pete found he was terribly conscious of the time, continually glancing at his watch. Finally, as they returned to the trailer from a trip to Marine World the next day, he was almost relieved. One-fifteen. For he never doubted his right to speak at exactly 1:37, and he wanted to get it over with.

The wait had not been as bad as expected. There was a lot to do in the trailer court. He and Barney had gone swimming, played pool, and last night they'd gone to a dance in the recreation room. In fact, the girls had asked *them* to dance. They'd been heroes just because they'd worked in a carnival. And what an act Barney had put on for them—the glories of working in a floss wagon, the excitement of the robbery, the responsibility of teardowns, and the glamour of being on the road! Not a word about losing his pay or wanting to quit every day he was there. In fact, Pete noticed the dice hadn't appeared since they hit Miami, and he wondered why. Was it the trip to the police station, or had Lily said something that made him put them away? Maybe she had flushed them down the toilet.

Pete stuck his hand in his pocket and felt the crisp fifty-dollar bill Lily had slipped him as they left for Marine World in the morning, saying she didn't want Barney owing him money for the best lesson he'd ever learned. So Barney *must* have told her the straight story.

Pete slid in the breakfast nook and sat looking out the window. There must be hundreds of trailers in the court, but each was so surrounded by hibiscus and palms and overgrown with vines that every space was like having your own private tropical garden. Through the open window he could hear the far-off sounds of television and families talking. Even the clatter of lunch dishes had a homey sound. It wouldn't be a bad place to live. He already felt more comfortable here than any other place he'd ever lived. And that was the trouble. It was like taking a tranquilizer. If he stayed much longer, he'd *never* get to the Virgin Islands.

Gradually Pete became aware of the silence inside the trailer. He looked up and found both Barney and Lily staring at him. "Did I miss something?" he asked, stalling for time now that it had run out.

"Oh, we were just talking about the goldfish pond Lily made from a dishpan. She even glued rocks all over the inside so the fish would feel at home." Barney laughed, and the laughter died in his voice.

"Only place goldfish feel at home is a muddy pond," Pete said.

"There's one in every crowd," sighed Lily, giving Pete a brief hug. "But I'll forgive you considering what

134

you taught me—or tried to—about your fishy friends this morning. Maybe we could go again and see the wing we missed—finish up. I always liked sea horses, and we missed them."

"I always liked sea horses, too," Pete said quietly. "Maybe. I thought I might check in at the airlines first and see when there's a flight—" What a lousy way to blurt out about his leaving, but at least he'd said something. He wanted to say he'd *rather* stay, but then they'd really work him over. There was *nothing* he could say that would change anything.

"What's your hurry?" Barney asked, and there was a hard challenge to his voice. As if he were really asking, what's wrong with us?

"Sure you don't want to go by and take a look at the trailer—it's fifteen feet." Lily's voice trailed off.

"You know, Barney, I *was* heading for the Virgin Islands—I have this aunt and—"

"What's she look like? Come on, tell me. See, you don't even know. Pete, give it up. It's nuts, a daydream!" Barney leaned forward, his face as intent as it had been the night Pete had watched him shooting craps.

Pete felt close to tears. They really wanted him! They weren't just being polite. He shook his head. "Barney, you're the best friend I've ever had. This is the first place —I'd like to stay. Really. But I have to go on, maybe just to see what it's like because I've been thinking about it so long. I don't know why, Barney, but it doesn't have much to do with what my aunt's like—more that she's *there*. Can't you understand that, at least?"

"I got three aunts and don't care if I never see them in my life."

"You've got Lily!"

135

"So could you."

"Simmer down, both of you. Pete's made up his mind. That's it. Now, let's go by the airline ticket office and the laundromat—we can't let Pete take off looking like a hooligan," Lily said, beginning to wash the dishes.

Pete sighed. He knew Lily was making it easy but, somehow, he was a little hurt. Maybe she didn't really care. He watched while she squirted too much liquid detergent into the tiny double sink and had to scoop soapsuds out of one into the other and then run cold water on them for some time before she could run rinse water.

"I keep telling you. Put in the detergent *after* you run the water and the suds won't go to the top—"

"Barney. You mind your own business—" Lily shouted. Her eyes looked moist, and her face was flushed.

"Here, let me do those," Barney said, grabbing the dishcloth. "We'll never get out of here, at all."

"Barney's a real homebody," Lily said, lifting one eyebrow in a gentle teasing Pete was coming to associate with her.

Barney did the dishes, and Lily dried and, for a while, no one said anything. Pete had a funny sinking feeling in the stomach, seeing them together and knowing this might be the last day he'd ever see them. Of course, he planned to look them up when he came back but, so far, that had never worked out with anyone else he'd liked.

"Well," Lily said, finally. "My grandfather was a first mate when he was twenty-one years of age. I suppose he must have been at sea by the time he was fifteen—if not earlier—would have had to be, don't you suppose? I wasn't much older when I got married, come to think of it, not that I'd recommend *that*." She kept shaking her head and shrugging as she put away dishes.

"Well, I guess there's no stopping you, is there?" She looked straight into Pete's eyes.

"I've got to go." He shook his head, and his smile was sad.

"I'll bet your aunt's dead. Otherwise, you'd phone her," Barney said and ran out of the trailer.

Pete held open the door and called after him. "They don't have phones on islands. That's why I haven't called," he yelled, knowing he could never have called. He stood there in the open doorway squinting his eyes against the glare. Barney had disappeared so he wasn't really looking *at* anything, just letting the hot air into the trailer and staring off into nothing. He knew he had to leave right away if he *was* going. Barney would be mad until he did, and he'd feel lousy, and Lily would be going around pricing trailers. He closed the door gently.

"I don't see why everything has to get so *complicated*," Pete said under his breath.

"I wish I had a quarter for everytime I've said that over the last fifty years." Lily laughed, but her voice sounded sad. "Let me finish the dishes, and we'll go get that ticket before you lose the cash down a manhole or something."

Seventeen

Only yesterday morning he'd been in the Miami airport, waving good-bye to Lily and Barney. Barney had sulked around the trailer until the last, not willing to see him off; but as Lily started the car, he'd come slamming out and climbed in. Then later Barney had said the thing that stuck in Pete's mind: that he couldn't understand why Pete and Lily both had to be always pushing on, leaving one place the minute they knew anyone to go on to somewhere strange. Pete had said that maybe they were just born wanderers. The words had sounded fine then, but now, twenty-four hours later, they had a flat ring to them.

Pete sat clutching the arms of his seat as the plane circled, waiting its turn to land at Truman Airport, St. Thomas, U.S. Virgin Islands. They'd been circling a long time. Maybe they'd run out of gas. Maybe something was wrong with the landing gear.

He forced himself to look down, through all the cloud

layers, down through the almost infinite thickness of the sky, to the intense blue below. He reminded himself again that that was still his ocean, with a school of dolphins probably following the wedge he knew must be a ship. But something had changed. Since he'd been in this plane, he knew the ocean was *really* only the floor to the sky.

He wanted to talk about the sky or ask why they kept circling, to get it out in the open, but his seatmate was asleep and the couple across the aisle were busy gathering their belongings for the landing. He stared at the woman as she carefully colored her lips orange with a brush. She seemed intent, as if the outline of her lips was the most important project in the world, and Pete felt like jerking her head around to the window so she'd *see* what was happening to them.

And then, suddenly, they started dropping. His stomach fell too as they lost altitude. It was such a little plane. And the runway was just a ribbon running between the mountains and the sea. They'd miss and land in the sea for sure. They'd overshoot, they'd *have* to overshoot! That's why they were dropping so fast.

Pete held on tight, trying to remember the instructions for emergency landings, and waited for the loud-speaker. He wondered if he should wake the man next to him but the man had on his seat belt and would crash-land more relaxed if he slept, so Pete did nothing. Then, gradually, he looked around at the other passengers, and no one else seemed worried at all. Remembering that this was only the second landing he'd ever made, he reminded himself sternly that he didn't know anything about it.

"Fasten your seat belts for landing, no smoking please." The girl's voice on the loudspeaker was crisp and routine.

The plane bumped again and again and ground to a motor-revving stop. They were on the ground, and in front of them was a huge corrugated iron shed with an enormous sign reading TRUMAN AIRPORT. They'd landed safely.

Then it was quiet. The silence was puzzling, until Pete realized that it was only that all the people had stopped talking. They were reaching overhead for coats and under seats for bundles and small suitcases. Then, as suddenly as it stopped, a babble of talking in several languages started again.

"Wait until the plane is fully stopped and the seat belt sign has gone off before leaving your seats, please. No smoking, please. We hope you have had a pleasant trip and thank you for flying Caribair." The stewardess repeated everything in Spanish and then in some other language that Pete guessed might be French.

"First flight, kid?" the man next to him asked with a midwestern drawl.

"Yes. How about you?" He let go of his grip on the arms of the seat, self-consciously.

"I fly over from Puerto Rico for golf once or twice a week. Just time for eighteen holes, and I can generally catch the noon flight back."

"Thirty bucks round trip," Pete whispered.

"Yeah, it's high, but one thing San Juan doesn't have is a decent golf course. Well, good luck," the big man said, hoisting himself out of the seat and joining the crowd in the aisle.

He should have asked the man what he did for a living. He probably wouldn't *ever* meet anyone with that much money again.

Pete sat quietly in his seat while everyone else was jostling and pushing to get out. He saw his seatmate standing with three other fat men claiming their golf bags from the stewardess beside the plane. Then he checked to make sure he had the claim for his backpack, felt for his wallet, and pulled his jacket from the rack overhead.

Something curious was taking hold of him as he sat watching people file past him. First his legs began to shake, and it was no sure thing that he would be able to stand and walk down that aisle. Then a muscle on the right side of his mouth began to twitch involuntarily, and he could not control it.

At the same time a sense of wonder was sinking in. He was there, in the airport at St. Thomas. He would walk out of this plane and talk to people who had lived on the island all their lives, and then he would walk down to the beach and dive into the Caribbean. He'd made it. He'd done it, really done it. They'd said he couldn't, but he had, he'd done it! Whatever else might happen all the rest of his life, he'd accomplished this one thing. He'd left Sebastopol in California heading for the Virgin Islands and he'd made it all by himself. And he was never going back, either.

Pete wasn't prepared for the rush of hot moist air as he stepped down the runway. Like walking into an oven and only 8:30 in the morning. It was going to take some getting used to. By tomorrow morning it would be easier and he'd be rested, which would help.

He hadn't gotten a lot of sleep last night, though considering everything, it hadn't been too bad. He'd gotten into San Juan Airport at 11 P.M., and the first thing he found out was that it would cost another twenty-five bucks to fly on to St. Thomas. The second shocker had been that there was no plane out until the morning and the cheapest room in the airport hotel was twenty-two dollars, which was almost two days' pay in the carnival. So he'd stretched out on a slat bench and slept in the Puerto Rico airport. He'd seen the guard take shoes off two sleeping men, so he'd taken off his own and put them in the pack under his head. All the guard *could* do was rap him across the feet with his billy as he came by every hour. Otherwise nobody bothered him. He'd been a little nervous though and came to like a shot every time the guard entered the waiting room. No matter. As soon as he collected his gear, he would go take a nap on the beach before hunting a room. And he still had almost a hundred dollars, thanks to Lily and skipping the hotel room.

The St. Thomas airport was out of some third-rate spy movie. It looked more like the inside of some huge corrugated-aluminum packing shed, more like the shed where he'd worked cutting apricots last summer than it did like the airports in Miami and San Juan. Each airline had a small glass cubicle and these ran along two sides of the building. The far end was open and filled with old taxis, station wagons, small hotel buses, and dilapidated jeeps. Beyond the cars ran a road and on the far side of that road the underbrush began. At least that was the way he had imagined it.

Huge overhead fans squeaked so loudly that there was no possbility of hearing the commands that came over the loudspeaker. It wasn't only the fans and the loudspeaker. The din of people talking, singing, and laughing was incredible. He did pick out a few words, and they seemed to be English. Pete had never seen so many black people before or, for that matter, so many tourists loaded down with so much luggage. Everyone else was picking up luggage and loading it into cars and buses and being taken off somewhere, and only Pete stood in the middle of this strange chaos wondering what to do next. He knew he'd made plans for today, but he could not remember anything. Everyone appeared to be smiling, but no one smiled at him.

He was hungry. The smell of pineapple hung over the moist hot air, probably from the juice people were drinking out of small cans. But if he didn't get his pack first maybe they'd send it back to San Juan along with the golf clubs. He spotted the luggage check-out down at the far end near the taxis and headed toward it, threading his way between hot bodies.

He held up his baggage check.

"Thisbeforyourownself, mon?" the attendant asked, pointing to a large gray suitcase.

"No, mine's a backpack, canvas with a sleeping bag tied on." He guessed at what the clerk wanted, looking over the mounds of luggage hopelessly. There was no telling where his pack might be.

"So then this beforyouentirely?" The suitcase wasn't his, but Pete was beginning to find the voice vaguely familiar from Calypso records he'd loved, but in whch he'd never bothered about the words. He pointed to the numbers on the check, and the clerk brightened and went off to look again. Pete leaned wearily on the counter. If *only* he could get breakfast and a swim, he'd be able to cope with the language. Airports were always bad. A black stranger at least seven feet tall was talking excitedly to Pete.

"Please, I don't understand. What do you want?"

"Kindly do not trouble yourself about that. And are you for needing transport to Redhook?" the man asked *very* slowly.

Pete shook his head. Wherever it was, he wasn't looking for transport, just for his backpack. The stranger stood a moment considering and then, just as Pete spotted his pack and sleeping bag over in one corner, he melted into the crowd.

"There, over there!" Pete called with enormous relief, spotting his pack. That gear and a hundred dollars were absolutely all he had in the world.

The attendant handed the pack to Pete with a great smile. The smile gradually faded as Pete took the bag, thanked him, and turned away. Pete wondered if he should have tipped him. Probably, but how much? The smallest he had was a five-dollar bill, and he didn't know if you could ask for change. Tomorrow he had to get a job first thing.

Still, the memory of that fading smile bothered him. It blended with the heat, the whirring fans, and the smell of sweat and decaying pineapple, the overwhelming sense of too many people. He felt caked in dust, nauseous, and uncertain what to do next. When he had thought of the Virgin Islands, he had always seen himself on some deserted beach. Not this!

People were beginning to look at him disapprovingly, as they pushed past. They resented young people in backpacks because they had no money and stole the pineapples. They could keep their old pineapples. The smell was bad enough.

Still, he *should* eat. Pete started toward the stairs but

couldn't make up his mind to start up. It was a steep stairway, and he couldn't think of anything he could keep down once he got to the restaurant at the top. Maybe a couple of soft-boiled eggs? It would be better to swim first, but how would he ever find his way to the beach?

"For Christ's sakes, make up your mind, boy. You're blocking the whole damn stairway!"

Pete whirled to face an angry man with a valpack over one arm. There were other people behind him. They looked mad, too.

"Oh, I'm really sorry!" he said, backing out of the way and looking around desperately for some refuge. He stood a moment and then backed under the stairway, shrugging out of his pack and sitting down, leaning gradually back against the pack.

He heard the man climb the stairs above him, his wife's high heels pounding like hammers on the metal stairway. Every woman here is fat, he thought, every single one of them.

"It would be different if Barney were here," he said aloud. "Barney always knows what to do." But that brought back Barney's words. "That aunt of yours is probably dead," he'd said. Barney would be *delighted* to see the mess he'd gotten himself into, crouching under the stairs like an alley cat. But Pete did not get up. Instead, he forgot Barney. Overhead footsteps pounded and gradually he did not hear them anymore, either.

Eighteen

Pete sat behind the stairwell, resting his back against the convolutions of the aluminum wall for a long while. From time to time the wind or a bump would shake the wall and rock him gently. At first he felt nothing else. It was soothing there, and he did not want to move. No one noticed him, back in the shadow.

Eventually he knew that he must move, must rent a room and take a swim before dark. He glanced at his watch and saw he'd been sitting there almost two hours. Soon. But not quite yet. He was here. He was on his own. That *was* what he wanted, wasn't it?

"Your aunt's probably dead," Barney had said, and earlier, "Don't count so much on an aunt who never did do more than send you a card once a year." And even as he sat under the stairwell telling Barney's memory that he'd come to the Virgin Islands for marine biology, not to pester an aunt he didn't know, he realized that Barney *had* understood what he was about. He wanted to see the fish, all right, but he also wanted to see if he had a family. He shivered and broke into a cold sweat. Possibly this was the stupidest thing he'd ever done in his life. Among other things, it was purely asking to be kicked in the teeth, which Barney had been trying to warn him.

Maybe the smartest move would be to catch the plane back to Florida. He still had just about enough money. Barney and Lily would be surprised, but they'd be happy to see him. His aunt would never know he'd been here, tracking her down. But even as he thought about leaving, Pete knew he would not. And with that knowledge, he began a plan. What he *did* have to do was to get a room, something to eat, and go for a swim, in that order. Tomorrow he could start looking for a job. The first thing was to find a bus into town, into Charlotte Amalie. He wanted a room right in the center of things, at least until he got a job.

Pete just managed to squeeze into the bus and drop his quarter in the box. The driver held up a fifty-cent piece, and Pete put another quarter in. Then the bus bounced off on a narrow gutted back road that kept opening onto views of the sea. Green hills and wild valleys ran back to the center of the island, and here and there Pete could see ruins of old plantation houses, overgrown with flowering vines. He was going to get a closer look at those, he decided, and soon.

The road was curving and dusty; and since the day was hot, every window in the bus stayed open so that passengers soon had a layering of dust. This didn't seem to bother anyone else. The passengers chattered in melodious voices, laughing often, but Pete could understand very little. No one paid much attention to him except to smile if he looked their way. He couldn't get over the feeling of having stepped into the *Arabian Nights*. He had known life would be different here, and he'd seen pictures of St. Thomas, but nothing had prepared him for either the astonishing beauty or the language.

As they bumped toward town, clusters of small houses overwhelmed by tiny but lush vegetable gardens gradually gave way to streets of houses, and Pete peered anxiously at his map. He wanted to get off at Dronningens Gade, but he noticed that the driver seldom called the streets and he had no hope of understanding if he did call Dronningens Gade. Without much hope he turned to an old black man sitting across the aisle and pointed to the street on his map.

"You will find Dronningens Gade to be the stop after next," the man said precisely, with an English accent. He smiled, and Pete grinned.

He was still grinning as he stepped down from the bus onto the cobblestones in front of an arcade of pink and yellow stucco shops. Dronningens Gade street lay in the busiest part of town, and no breeze penetrated its rows of two-story stone buildings. The afternoon sun beat down fiercely. Pete felt the sweat rolling underneath his pack. It was the hour of the siesta, and the street was almost empty of cars or people. Pete loved the street on sight and determined to find a room as close as possible.

Only after he had found one, dank, small, and more than he could pay but the cheapest he ran across, did he allow himself to approach the post office with his aunt's address. And then it was late afternoon before Pete finally got to the quiet beach where he learned she still lived. There were several houses among the palms and mahoe trees and sea grape that grew in a tangle from the white sand beach up the steep island, and he made no effort to guess which was hers. He walked quickly across the beach, and, dropping his towel, dove into the warm surf. This was more like it, he thought, turning on his back and looking up at the clear sky.

If only everything didn't cost so much. The bus had been fifty cents and the pineapple and orange he had bought from a fruit stand for lunch had cost a dollar and a half, about three times what they'd have charged in Miami. He felt a cold fear that he might starve on this lush island. God knew, the foster homes he'd lived in hadn't been much and were very easy to forget, but he'd never in his life worried that he might not have enough to eat. He did now—in paradise. Pete smiled at the irony. If he was careful, he could keep his room and eat for the next week. One week.

He rolled over on his stomach and stroked slowly through the warm water, stopping occasionally to turn on his back and look up into the sky. A pair of pelicans circled overhead, smaller and leaner than California brown pelicans, with deep turquoise underwings. The turquoise *had* to be a reflection of the sea. And even as he knew this, the pelicans turned in the midst of a graceful arc and dove into the sea. One surfaced instantly with a fish about the size of a perch in his mouth, possibly a grouper. He gulped the fish to the pouch in his throat and dove again. Another fish. Both pelicans had dinner. *They* didn't have to worry.

And, playfully, Pete dove and found himself in a school of small silverfish that scattered only slightly while he careened into their midst. He surfaced and shook out his wet hair and laughed. He could do anything a pelican could! He scanned the shore, beyond the rim of white sand, to the tangled growth around the half-dozen houses on the beach, reaching back into a kind of jungle, with coconut palms and mango trees. Orchids were pretty but not much to eat. Sea grape must be good for something though and there must be bananas somewhere, hot country like this. All those people on the bus couldn't pay the prices he'd seen. There wouldn't be any problem about getting cold, so he wouldn't need many clothes. He'd make it. He could survive here.

Just as long as he could float around in this water all day—without rip tides or much seaweed—swimming with fish the colors of the rainbow, he'd be just fine.

Gradually Pete found the fish were not his only company. Another swimmer, more like a cavorting dolphin, was bouncing along in his general direction. The swimmer, a girl, kept diving to the bottom and coming up blowing water, spinning, and then diving again. She might be snorkeling, except that she had neither mask nor fins. Even wet he could tell her hair was long and blond, and it occurred to him that this could be his cousin. She'd had long straight hair in the last couple of Christmas cards, and this *was* the beach where she lived, after all. He treaded water and waited. She wouldn't be expecting him for tea, after all. He didn't have to tell her who he was. She might not recognize the name, even if he did.

"Hey, watch out for the sea anemones," she said. "They're heavy today—the big tide last night brought a whole bellyful and they have stingers that will swell your feet like you've got elephantiasis. Do you know one when you see it?"

150

"Did you come all the way out here just to tell me *that?*"

"Never mind then," she said, without rancor, and dove again. When she surfaced, Pete grinned.

"Hey, I didn't mean to put you down. I was surprised because it was such a good thing to do, coming to warn me."

"Well, you looked like a stranger when you came down to our beach, so I was afraid you mightn't know—"

"What do you mean, your beach?" Pete was trying to decide if she looked like him, this girl who might be his cousin. She was tall and lean and had green eyes, which he did, but her features didn't add up like his. Her face was fuller and shorter or something strange. She was good looking, it wasn't that. But it was as if you could describe them and people would say there was a similarity, but you wouldn't say they were from the same family if you saw them face to face. Probably more than one blond on this beach, anyhow. She was just a kind stranger.

"We live right over there. I've lived on the island all my life, though not in that awful house, I'm happy to say."

"Awful?" The house she'd indicated was definitely the best on the beach, a large natural rock house with a wide veranda and surrounding palms and tropical growth so that it seemed to be coming out of the jungle. Hibiscus and bougainvillea climbed all over one side. It was a dream, that house.

"Oh, it's haunted," she said airily.

"You're kidding!"

"OK. Maybe, I just never lived anyplace that was so much work, and *that* haunts me."

Pete stared. He wanted to ask her name, but he couldn't. It was too important. Instead, he asked, "Am I trespassing—using the beach?"

"Only right out in front of the house is ours, and we don't care as long as you don't leave beer cans all over." The girl dove down into the water, sinewing through to the bottom as if she were a fish. Pete felt dismissed. He'd missed his chance to ask her name.

Then she shot up a few yards away and easily swam back to him. She was grinning.

"You don't even need snorkeling stuff. I've never seen anyone hold their breath so long," he said, smiling.

"If you didn't have anything else to do your whole life *but* swim, you'd learn too. I'm tired of treading water —want to go in?" she asked over her shoulder as she swam for shore. She used a strong sure stroke, no dolphin antics this time, and Pete made no pretense of trying to keep up with her.

"Over to your left, by the black coral. *That's* an anemone!" she yelled as Pete waded out of the surf. It was the first time in his life he'd climbed out of the ocean without a cold shock, so he shook and stretched before he glanced over to where she was frantically pointing. Three anemones lay in a clump, like three delicate blue-black shells about the size of abalone. He had half a mind to tell this bossy girl more about anemones than she'd find out in her lifetime, but he hesitated. Showing off had lost him friends before, and he didn't even know who she *was* yet.

"I know," he compromised.

"I'm Becky Taylor, by the way. Are you going to be here long? Where you from?" She sat cross-legged in the sand, her gray eyes friendly.

Pete knew he was staring. He saw her shift uneasily, and with an effort tore his eyes away. So she *was* his cousin. She was the first relative he'd seen since he was five, this Becky Taylor. He tested to see what he felt— but it seemed to be only shock. Maybe it took a while, this feeling people were supposed to have about relatives.

"I'm Pete Logan." He waited to see if she recognized him. He could always claim he just had the same name.

"Glad to meet you, Pete. You down for the summer?"

The name Pete Logan meant nothing to her, luckily. Still, it did show that they sure didn't spend their evenings wondering how he was. Had his aunt even told this cousin he existed? Maybe she was ashamed because of the foster homes. She had been his father's sister. Maybe they hadn't gotten along.

"Are you down for the summer?" she asked again, impatiently.

"I guess." Pete didn't want to lie, but he wasn't about to go into his life story either. Not yet. He slapped at something stinging his arm.

"Sand flies. Slapping won't help."

"Oh?" She seemed to think she was the absolute authority on everything. Then Pete caught his breath. That's what Johnny and his father said about *him*. Maybe it was inherited, bossiness. They couldn't both be that way because they were cousins, could they? This being a cousin was like looking in a mirror.

"Not a chance. You just have to endure them until they get tired or you get immune. Come on over to the house and we'll spray you with Off and that will keep most of them away, for a while, anyway." Becky got up slowly, without bothering to brush off sand.

"No, thanks. It was just that one. Can anyone go snorkeling on these reefs?" Pete asked, anxious to change

153

the subject. The very last thing in the world he wanted was to go over to that house and get sprayed. The flies kept biting, but he would have died rather than slap again and give that girl, Becky, his cousin, the chance to drag him over—scratching—

"Oh, sure. I'll take you tomorrow, if you like, Pete. I don't have anything else to do."

"Great, except I don't have fins and mask yet. I guess there's—"

"We've got enough for an army. Come on now, and we'll spray—"

Pete shook his head emphatically. The flies were killing him, but that was no way to meet his aunt. He looked longingly at the water. "Look, can I meet you tomorrow? I've got to get back to town now. I want to see about a job." He stood up so he was facing the girl, his cousin.

"Boy, *that's* the scarcest thing on the island. You're *lucky* if you can get a job."

"I'm thinking about commercial fishing."

"*What* commercial fishing—darn little—only the groupers and turtles right now—are you in the union?"

"Not yet." He felt as if he were lying, both by hinting he had a lead on a job and by not telling her that he was her cousin; but he couldn't do that, somehow. Not yet. He had to go back to his room and let this Becky, who was also somehow a part of him, seep in first. Besides, he felt as if he were breaking out in hives.

"Tomorrow?" he asked.

"Sure. I'll be here with the snorkeling stuff."

She seemed deflated, let down, somehow, as if he'd brushed her off, and Pete yearned to sit down and tell her everything. Instead he smiled, waved, and headed back up the sand to the path leading away from the beach. At the top, just before he entered a tunnel cut through the tangle of sea grape, he turned.

"Hey, Becky, don't forget," he called.

She grinned and waved, and ran off toward her house.

He started to scratch as soon as he was out of sight.

Nineteen

Later that night, Pete lay on the bed in the room he'd rented, looking up at the sluggish clanking fan, feeling his stomach turn and catch in the rhythm of the fan. Everything smelled of mildew and the heavy sweet frangipani flowers that covered his window, obscuring what breeze there might be so the room was a dank hot cave. He'd sprayed himself with an entire can of insecticide, which he found cost two dollars, and still the sand flies bit. His arms, legs, and face were swollen and aching. Dully he wondered if this had caused his nausea or if it were the memory of his cousin and the certainty that, through her, he would see his aunt. There was no turning back.

He'd been in St. Thomas fourteen hours, less than a day, and he knew his life would never be the same again, not only because he'd met Becky, though that was the big change. It was also that the island was so different from any place he'd ever lived or dreamed about, hot and muggy for the first thing. No one would ever think of pole vaulting or playing football in this weather. And his very thinking seemed to sift through layers of heat, so that he couldn't think through to the end and make a decision about anything.

But there was more than the heat. This was a strange place. Everything, everything was so bright it seemed almost fluorescent. The sea had to be the most brilliant blue in the world, and the sky, the flowers, and the fish matched it in intensity. No wonder the tourists all went around in dark glasses. And the way people talked, like a foreign country. He could lie still and, over the fan, he could hear people outside the window laughing and talking softly, like music, an exciting sound. But he'd never understand a word if he lived to be a hundred, even though they were speaking English.

It wouldn't be so bad if Barney were here. Pete felt he ought to write him. He'd promised to write the first day. At least it would keep his mind off the sand flies. He rummaged in the top drawer of the little desk. The creamy sheets of letter paper even had a crest, which made it seem like a real hotel. Maybe he'd write Carl, too.

A breeze came up, and he could hear the palms slapping and the smell of the pink frangipani blended with salt from the sea. Perhaps he could walk down and look at the boats after he finished his letters. That's what he'd do and he'd stay as long as he wanted. He could even stay *all night* and watch the fishing boats go out before dawn if he wanted. It was no one's business but his own, anymore.

It was the next afternoon before Pete brushed through the mahoe branches and sea grape, and made his way to

Becky's beach with a mixture of assurance and trepidation. On the one hand he was getting his bearings on the island. He'd spent last night and the morning wandering around town, and he was beginning to understand the lilting speech. He found he liked the people. They had a good time, and they were friendly.

He'd also gone to the employment agency, and that had been less successful. The men at the agency thought he was kidding when he asked for a job. He was white; therefore he must be rich. Nevertheless, he'd filled out an application and watched where the clerk tossed it. The dust of months rose when his application hit the foot-high pile!

At the moment he was afraid Becky might be gone. They hadn't set a time, but he was probably *much* later than she had expected. *If* she hadn't forgotten completely about the snorkeling.

But he saw her lying on the beach reading, two snorkels and masks on the sand beside her. He noticed with some relief that she hadn't brought tanks. He hadn't mentioned that he didn't know how to use them yet.

Pete stood so that his shadow fell on her book and waited. She finished the page, turned it, and finished the next before she looked up.

"Mad?" he asked.

She shook her head and smiled. "We never set a time. How do you feel?"

"Like I've been walking around in the *Arabian Nights.*"

"Well, you *look* like you've got chicken pox. Those sand flies really think you're juicy. I think we'd better go up to the house and get some tranquilizers into you!"

"Tranquilizers? Not on your life. Come on, the water will help."

158

"Not enough. Not the way you've been scratching. Look, Pete, people land in the hospital from these bites— the capsules we have keep you from itching—now, don't be stupid!" Becky got up and, without bothering to gather her book or the masks and fins, headed toward the stone house.

Pete stood frozen. Then he sighed and, bending down, picked up his cousin's stuff and followed her. There was probably no point in putting it off, and he certainly couldn't risk landing in the hospital.

"Hey, wait a minute, Becky. There's something I've got to tell you!"

"It can wait. Come on."

"No, it can't. I'm your cousin!"

Becky turned then and stared at him. Pete thought she must be trying to see if they looked alike, just as he had the day before. She didn't look pleased, and Pete shifted uneasily.

"Oh, which one?" she asked, finally.

"What do you mean, *which* one?" Pete called after her.

Becky turned. There were tears in her eyes. "Every single time I meet a new boy, someone interesting, it turns out he's my relative—you're at least the fifth cousin who's showed up—all boys. They think the islands are *so* free, *so* romantic, and then they take their tans and go back stateside at the end of the summer. Everyone leaves in September. I spend nine months of the year by myself. Stop scratching! Come on—let's do something about your scratching before you tear your legs to shreds." She turned and walked across the white sand toward the house.

Pete sprinted after her and took her hand. Gradually he felt her relax. He was tempted to tell her he wouldn't leave in September but hesitated. When they reached the front steps, he dropped her hand and turned.

"You're the first relative I've had—I got to go now. I'd like to clean up first—before I tackle my aunt—maybe tomorrow," Pete said quietly.

"Oh—come on! She won't bite. It's better *this* way. Wipe the sand off your feet." Becky's voice was gentle. Then she stepped onto the veranda and called loudly. "Mo-ther, company!"

"I can hear you. So can your father on the other side of the island."

Pete looked up, and the woman on the Christmas card stood in the doorway. His aunt. His throat was dry. He might pass out. She didn't look like him at all, not even the way Barney and Lily looked like each other. Maybe it was all a mistake. But she didn't look like Becky, either. She was little and dark, and she didn't look old enough to be Becky's mother. She didn't look like *anyone's* mother. And still, she looked familiar. Pete decided it was because she looked like women he'd seen in magazines—the wife of some famous guy or other. And the smile on her face was tentative, like theirs, as if she wasn't sure she wanted any. But the main thing was, she was too young.

"Hello there," she said. She had a drink in one hand, and she set it on a window ledge as she came toward them.

"Pete Logan, meet my mother—and your Aunt Lemore!" Becky was obviously enjoying the scene.

"Pete—Logan—Johnny's boy?"

"I guess." Was she talking about *his* father? Nobody ever had. He remembered coming home from school—kindergarten, everyone there had parents—and asking what happened to his. The matron said she'd heard they were killed in an accident. He'd never asked again, and no one had said anything more, either. He probably should have written and asked his aunt when she sent Christmas cards. Or let it alone. He'd been doing all right. What was he doing here? She didn't look all that glad to see him, either.

"You *are* Peter Logan?"

He nodded.   He used to spend hours hunting for a card to send her every Christmas.

"Well, then." She put her arms out and he moved gingerly into them. She smelled of perfume, and he remembered Lily, the only other lady who'd put her arms around him. But these arms were tense, holding him still, and he was relieved when it was over.

His aunt held him off, looking. "Why didn't you write? Well, boys don't. You're the spitting image of your father. I'd know you anywhere, Pete. It's almost spooky. I haven't seen Johnny since he left home when I was eight—but you are a dead ringer for him, no mistake about that. He never could get along with my daddy—not many could—and I never saw him again, nor ever met your mother either, I'm afraid. Well, come on in and tell us how you got here—edge of the world for you. Becky—get the medicine before this boy scratches himself raw." She sank into a rattan chair and lit a cigarette. studying him.

Pete was shaking. He wished she'd keep on talking. She had a great husky voice. As if she heard his unspoken wish, his aunt turned to Becky and told her he'd come from California, was her half brother's son and that she'd always hoped they'd get together one day. He half-heard all this, but he knew only one thing. He had to get out of there. He had to be by himself for a while and think.

"Where are you staying?" he heard his aunt ask.

"Pete needs a job—I think—or did you get one?"

He shook his head. If he didn't get out he might throw up right here.

"Ever done any gardening, Pete? You're welcome to stay with us—for a while—you *are* down for the summer? Becky could use a playmate—wouldn't ride me so hard —"

His stomach flip-flopped. He saw Becky's face go white at the playmate crack.

"We usually hire one of the boys to garden, and you might as well—" Aunt Lenore spoke in short low phrases, and Pete wasn't sure he was being offered a job or room and board. He didn't feel well enough to ask, that much was certain.

"You wrote on that last card you wanted to be a marine biologist—that still the big push?"

He nodded.

"Doesn't everybody?" Becky laughed.

Pete flushed. "Please, Aunt, can I come back tomorrow? I've got to go now." The smell of the insecticide stuck in his throat, and he couldn't even remember his aunt's name.

"Aren't you staying for dinner, even?" Becky asked as he fled, stumbling down the rock steps and running across the beach, toward the covering of some bushes. He made it just in time.

Twenty

He regretted most of all, those next two days as he lay
in his room, that he and Becky had not gone snorkeling.
He would have enjoyed thinking over the fish, letting them
parade across his mind in colorful profusion. There was no
question of going later, since his legs turned to jelly every
time he tried to get out of bed. The first day he did drag
himself to the employment office where again they shrugged
and smiled. But on the way back, he kept seeing spots before his eyes, so he bought a bag of fruit and did not go out
again.

He did not know whether he had flu or a reaction
to knowing himself as Johnny's son—of seeing this woman
who had known his father and therefore gave him exist-
ence. Or perhaps he was sick from the bites that were
swelling into welts that puffed into each other and covered his body, in which case he would probably end up
in the hospital. Whatever, it felt luxuriously good to lie

under the creaking fan and doze, waking first to sunshine and later to a glimpse of stars through the frangipani vine and still later to morning again and the clusters of tiny yellow birds that pecked at the pink blossoms. Always there was the melodious hum of voices under his window, and he found this oddly soothing.

In fact, he did not feel bad so long as he stayed in bed. Terribly tired. Grateful to lie still. Too weary to decide whether to live with Aunt Lenore or, indeed, to plan at all. He drifted.

On the third morning he woke feeling wonderful. He was a little weak at first but, after a good breakfast, he was ready to go back and see his aunt. It occurred to Pete that she and Becky might be angry because he had not come back earlier but, if so, it was not likely he could do anything about that. He had a curious feeling, new to him, that he'd just wait and see what developed. If Aunt Lenore still wanted a gardener, he'd move in until he could find another job. If she did not, then he'd find what he could or scrounge the beaches if nothing else turned up. He was down to thirty dollars.

He found Becky alone on the beach again, two masks and fins still alongside her. She must spend her life on the sand, stretched out with her head in a book. There was something taut and expectant about her, as if she were waiting, and Pete half hoped she hadn't been waiting for him and half hoped she had. He stood awkwardly a few feet away, wondering what to say.

After he decided, Pete walked up and said, trying to sound casual, "I thought I *might* give that gardening job a try, if it's still open.

When Becky looked up, her smile took in her entire

face, as though Pete had made her particularly happy. "I'm glad. I was afraid mother had spooked you. It's a nasty habit she's gotten lately. What took you so long?"

Pete shrugged.

"Mom said it was probably withdrawal symptoms."

He laughed then because that was as good a way of describing the last two days as any. He wanted to make sure the gardening job was still open. He waited for Becky to say something about going on up to the house.

"Well," she said instead, "how about that snorkeling date we had?" The word *date* carried a faintly bitter accent.

"Two days late?"

"Three, but come on, better late than never, and the salt water will help dry up those bites."

"Maybe we should go up and say hello to Aunt Lenore first."

"She's napping. She said to bring you in time for dinner when you showed up—*if* you showed up."

"Ve-ry funny," Pete muttered, hurrying to keep up with Becky as she trotted across the hot sand toward a reef jutting out into the sea, dividing this beach from the one around the bend. The hot sand hurt his feet, and Pete really wanted to settle where he was going to stay tonight before swimming, but it looked as if Becky had been waiting a long while. Three days?

He picked up his snorkeling equipment and followed her. After all, what did it matter if he spent one more night in the hotel? He wouldn't need money once he came to live with his aunt. *Stay,* not live with them—just for a while. Still, he felt lighthearted.

Instead of diving in the water, Becky headed for the

reef that divided their beach from the next. They walked out on coral, which just broke the surface so that the blue water rippled around them, making soft gurgling sounds. Pete stepped gingerly over the gray-pink coral, remembering tales of infection, but Becky charged ahead out into the bay. The further they went, the deeper the color of the water to either side of them, which meant the reef dropped straight down, an underwater cliff. From the beach it must seem as if they were walking *on* water. He straightened his shoulders and stretched wide his arms, flapping lightly, to further the illusion.

Finally he looked deep into the water on either side of the narrow reef and caught his breath. They were walking right down the middle of a tropical aquarium, standing on a piece of coral in the middle of an enormous fishbowl, as if they were the tiny plastic figures that come in Cracker Jack boxes. And all around them the fish went on about their business. There were the groupers, of course, and parrot fish, the big lazy pompano, and a yellow-and-purple fish about the size and shape of an angelfish. Great schools of tiny silverfish swam through the others like streaks of light. He'd seen most of these fish in books, but pictures weren't the same as these darting shimmering beauties—nothing he'd *ever* seen had prepared him for their beauty.

"You don't really need anything else at all," he whispered.

"Hey, slowpoke, you're as bad as any old tourist." Becky had doubled back and knelt next to him. "Watch the parrot fish. He's a lopsided swimmer."

"I just can't believe *any* of them. Are there many reefs where they come?"

"Practically every single reef in the Caribbean," Becky

166

said proudly. "And further out you get the bigger fish. We have an old barracuda who has lolled around out at the end of the reef ever since I can remember."

"You act like he's an old friend, but I'll bet he'll take an arm or a leg if he gets a chance. In fact, that's probably what he's waiting around for."

"He's never hurt anyone so far—Daddy says he's probably vegetarian—OK, laugh—wait until you meet him— ever seen a squall—over to the left."

Pete turned to see it raining a few hundred yards away while they stood in the hot sun. As he watched, the rain moved, skirting the island and heading out to sea.

"Weird. It's like someone turned on one of those traveling sprinklers," he said.

"If you want to see real misery, look at a guy with an empty cistern when a squall just misses *his* place and hits his neighbor's garden. Come on, let's get going."

Pete wasn't nearly so eager to get in the water since hearing about the barracuda. In fact, there seemed little point when they could sit on the reef and watch more fish than he'd ever dreamed of seeing at once. All he wanted was to sit on this reef and look up into the clear sky and down into the water. He smiled wistfully at Becky, who was already strapping rubber fins on her feet. Good legs, Pete thought.

"Come on! What are you waiting for—a hurricane?"

"When will we have hurricanes?" he asked eagerly, drawing one hand lazily through the water, while fish swarmed around it.

"Any time now—come on!" She dove in, barely causing a ripple and her long blond hair floated fanlike over the surface.

Obediently Pete got into fins and goggles, and let

himself into the warm water. In a few minutes the fish accepted them, seeming curious. A grouper swam alongside him, moving eye to eye. "And here we were, this grouper and I, eyeballing each other, half a mile out," he could see himself writing to Barney.

At first, Pete tried to see every fish that darted from each crevice and sea fan, partly because he was worried about the barracuda. Gradually he let himself become a part of the scene, as if he were watching a light show, where the lights whirled endlessly and haphazardly and all you could do was catch hold somewhere and ride with them. Occasionally he and Becky would pull up onto the reef and rest a while, but neither made any attempt to talk during these times. They might wave. Becky must feel, as he did, the privilege of being with the fish.

This reef would be his study. He would come every day and try to know how these fish lived, what happened when the weather and the sea changed, the spawning, bearing, everything!

Once before, when he was about seven, he remembered adopting a red anthill. It was in the playground, and it must have been a holiday because he'd watched all day without being called back for chores. The worker ants had carried crumbled pieces of bread and a stick of bacon into the hill. They formed long lines like a safari. Never stopping, never hurrying. He remembered the smells of new green grass and steaming earth. Then—suddenly— a kickball had landed right in the middle of the hill. And then, as he sat there crying, he saw the ants crawling out of the crater that had been their hill and, re-forming their lines, rebuild. The following morning the hill was as conical as ever, its inhabitants steadily going about their business. Would he find the fish had communities like that?

Later, lying on the beach with Becky, Pete found himself telling her about the different places he'd lived, even Juvenile Hall. Her gray eyes grew wide and excited.

"Oh, I've always thought a juvenile hall must be the most fascinating place in the world, so *many* kids."

"Mostly hard work. We had to scrub and sometimes wax the floors before we went to school in the morning—and all the kids outside think you're a crook."

"Still," Becky said wistfully, "you got to know what different kinds of life are like—what it's like to live with different families. All I know is my own dull life."

"You know, that's just what my friend Barney said. I mean, I can't believe it. Almost the same words. But the truth is—" Pete paused because he'd never said this out loud to any other person. He saw Becky sitting with her hands folded, cross-legged, looking at him, waiting. "The truth is—that you're never a part of *any* family. You're always on the outside looking in." *Don't* let her say I'll be a part of *her* family, Pete thought.

Becky was quiet for a while, looking at her hands, spreading the fingers and making fists and spreading them again. "Well," she said, "that's how I've always felt, any-how—but it's not too bad, I guess. Come on, let's go tell Mom you're moving in—before she starts dinner." Becky jumped up in the quick way she had, and grabbing Pete's hands, pulled him up. "Race you to the house?"

Twenty-One

A few days later Pete heard Aunt Lenore tell a visitor that her latest shirttail nephew was settling in nicely. It didn't sound as if he was getting through to her very well, and he'd noticed his own tendency to keep thinking of her as Becky's mother rather than his aunt. Somehow, they'd never gotten back to that first afternoon where he'd been Johnny's son. He'd never even felt like asking about his father again, and she'd volunteered no information. In fact, his aunt did not appear to find him very interesting.

At the employment office, the clerks continued to think it hilarious that anyone living in a big house on the beach should be looking for work. Becky's parents wondered when he had to be back in California for school. So he told them September fifteenth, setting his own deadline for getting another job.

His nightmares had come back, a recurring dream in

which he fought seaweed—pushing, biting, straining against the dank sinews that turned out to be sheets every morning. Barney was in the dream now, rolling his dice and shaking his head. It was hard to get up in the morning after one of these nightly battles, and the heat didn't help. The trick was to get out in the garden before anyone noticed that he'd overslept. This led to the fiction that he didn't always feel like breakfast.

The garden was a jungle, which Pete, Becky, and Uncle Ray accepted. But Aunt Lenore was determined to grow roses and California poppies. Uncle Ray said that in the tropics this was like Don Quixote fighting windmills. He could be very funny, but Aunt Lenore was not the type to appreciate a joke, especially on her.

This particular morning Pete woke to hear them bickering in the garden. That meant breakfast must be over already. He was late. Maybe if he could grab something from the refrigerator and run for the back garden they might think he'd been working for hours.

He untangled himself from the sheets, pulled on shorts, and made a dash for the kitchen. The floor had just been mopped and the damp concrete felt good on bare feet, cool in the already humid morning. He wondered what time it was as he reached for the refrigerator door and pulled.

He screamed, and the sound of his voice terrified him more than the shock, more than not being able to let go of the refrigerator door. More than electricity itself. He felt he was losing consciousness, sinking down into the seaweed, sinking finally into a heap on the floor, still hearing his wild animal cries.

"What's wrong?"

Running feet. Too late. Running feet.

"For Christ sakes, sneaking in the refrigerator. If that isn't the limit," he heard Aunt Lenore say. "As if we don't feed him enough." Her voice sent the torturing shocks down his nerve endings again.

"He got quite a shock. We'd better get him to a doctor." Uncle Ray's voice was soft and low. A guitar.

"Uncle Ray. Don't touch. You'll—get caught!" He yelled, only then hearing in his natural voice that it was over. He was alive. He no longer held the refrigerator door. He lay huddled on the damp concrete floor and began pushing himself away from that lethal box, from the two sets of eyes staring down, like stars from a sky. He was alive.

"How often do I have to tell everyone they *must* wear zoris in this kitchen? These connections were never grounded right. Nothing on this damn island ever is. Are you all right, boy?"

He was crying, and they would think it was the electricity, but they were wrong. He *could* have said Pete, not boy. That wouldn't have taken much.

"What were you *doing* in the refrigerator?" Becky's mother's charm bracelet jangled, sending shivers up his spine.

"Oh, Lord, Lenore, he probably wanted a glass of milk! The boy's almost lost his life. If I hadn't thrown the master switch, I hate to think—"

"I got up late," Pete said.

"Well, you don't have to yell at me, Ray." She started to cry.

"Lenore, let's have one peaceful morning, just one."

He could see them glaring at each other, and it occurred to him that if he could only crawl out of the kitchen right then while they'd forgotten about him, he might disappear into the garden and, after he'd rested, crawl on out to the road.

"Can you move, boy? Should we get a doctor?"

It was too late. Impossible anyway as he could never have crossed the floor with each muscle aching and that strange tingling, as if his nerves were still drawn to the refrigerator. He felt nauseous. Aunt Lenore smelled of some sweet perfume that mixed badly with the Clorox on the floor and the rotting bananas, and he had to get away. He groped, stretching out one arm to crawl—

Uncle Ray picked him up and carried him out onto the deck, away from the bananas and the white box, and set him gently on a straw couch. Pete lay back and enjoyed the fresh air.

"I'll be all right now. I missed breakfast so I was just —going to get a sandwich—so I wouldn't bother you—" He felt the tears again, and turned his face away.

Just then Becky called out from the beach and started up toward the house. He could tell she'd been swimming and wished she'd go back. He could stand *anything* but her sympathy. It would be better to thank Uncle Ray and be done with it before she showed up.

"I guess you saved my life—thanks a lot," he said, remembering in bitterness the non-name, boy.

"My negligence, I suppose, when you get right down to it. Well, we were lucky, this time. Just you lie here, and Lenore will get you a decent breakfast."

Not willingly, he thought, shaking his head.

"I couldn't eat *anything*."

"Well, *I* could eat a horse. Who's for a pineapple

shake?" Becky gave him a casual glance and went on into the kitchen.

"Don't touch that refrigerator!" her mother yelled, running after her.

"Well, I'd better reground that and get it turned on again before Lenore bursts a blood vessel," her father sighed. "I don't suppose you happened to notice if Becky was wearing her zoris?"

"Yes, she was." He remembered them sucking at the concrete.

"What's going on around here?" Becky asked, facing them, hands on hips, her wet hair dripping on tan skin. Pete watched her mouth drop open as they told the story, Aunt Lenore blaming the faulty grounding instead of him in the retelling.

"Boy, are you brave," she whispered when they finished.

He was relieved that she said no more. Of course, bravery had nothing to do with accidentally getting shocked because he'd opened her mother's refrigerator door. That was hardly a question of choice. And then he thought that if it weren't for the accident of her mother *happening* to be his aunt, he wouldn't be bothering with any of these people. He would never have pulled that door. And suddenly he wanted to get away from them all.

"Is it all right if I go to my room for a while before I weed?"

"Forget the garden. Rest. I give you a holiday!" Uncle Ray said with a sweep of his arm.

Later that afternoon Pete and Becky went into town. By that time he'd gotten used to walking, and the headache was gone. Only a curious ache remained, so that he was conscious of each muscle individually, causing him to examine himself as if he were a crab or a lobster.

"It's like being a plastic man," he told Becky as they waited for mail at the general delivery window of the post office.

"I wish you *were* a little transparent," she replied.

But Pete was busy opening letters from Barney and Lily, and did not listen. A ten-dollar bill fell out of the latter.

"Wow! You're lucky. Nobody but my grandma *ever* writes to me."

"Does she send you ten-dollar bills?" He'd started to suggest that Barney would answer if she wrote, and realized he didn't want them writing each other. However, he did hand Becky Barney's letter.

Dear Pete,

Did you know the average age in Miami is sixty-three years old? I've about given up hope that you'll be back—from what you say the people there are almost as great as the fish—so I'm saving my dough to come to VI next summer. Too bad, though, because it would have been great to have our own trailer, and they say the school here is big in track and all the fish stuff too. School starts Sept. 15 in case you change your mind. Everyone at the pool asks about you. I've got an easy job cleaning up the court, but it's full time so I'll have to find someone to split it with or quit when school starts. Bet you and I could have sewn it up. Carl comes through next week, and I'm not too hot on him and Lily having any heart-to-heart talk about you-know-what. Guess that's about all—write when you get the chance. I never was much good at writing, but I'll write back.

Barney

"Sounds like he misses you," Becky said. "What's he mean about you-know-what?"

"Lily—his grandmother, that is—wants me to come back, too," Pete said, with a rough bitterness that startled him.

Becky looked at him curiously, frowning. "What did he mean about you-know-what?"

"Gambling," Pete said, and fell silent, thinking about the trailer court, and meeting Lily; and how she stuck with him until the doctor was sure his arm wasn't hurt badly, and finally about Barney and his dice. Carl might already be with them. He'd have some tall tales to tell about how things were since they left the carnival. Pete scuffed along the hot sidewalk, trying to stick with Becky in the crush of people. Natives and tourists alike had arms bursting with packages. He felt terribly tired. If only he could be cold for half an hour. Where were those trade winds?

"Shall we go down to the dock?" he asked. It was already routine for them to sit, dangling their feet in the water, and talk with the fishermen.

"No," Becky said definitely. "Let's go get fruit salad at the Grand Hotel. We've both got money today, and we can celebrate your escape. You can look down on everyone's heads, and it's cool, and the tourists don't go there."

Pete had been about to refuse anything that cost money automatically; but if it was cool and there weren't tourists, he wanted to go. He needed to feel he belonged, at least to the island.

The Grand Hotel was an old Victorian, two-story fading yellow wood building that curved around one corner, bulging so that the second-story restaurant veranda looked as if it might fall on the crowded sidewalk it shaded. According to Becky, it had always looked that way; whether she meant as long as she could remember or for the hundred years this hotel had been there, she didn't say. Magnificent columns ran from the veranda to the street. They had once been painted white, but salt and wind had long since left them peeling and pleasantly colorless. For some reason the general shabbiness made the hotel a favorite meeting place for all permanent residents and discouraged tourists. Pete had never been there before, but felt instantly that if he were given a choice this veranda was the spot where he wanted to spend his first hurricane.

"Isn't it like a castle?" Becky said as they climbed the broad arching stairway to the veranda. Old beach drawings hung on the wall at each step.

"Disneyland's haunted house." Pete laughed.

"Look, we can turn right around and leave!" Becky stood, hand on hip, her gray eyes angry.

"Hey, I was just kidding. I think it's the greatest place I've ever been."

"Well, then *don't* kid." She stomped up the stairs.

"Oh, my favorite table," Becky said and headed for a small table by the rickety railing that overhung the street. A waitress started toward Becky as if she were about to show her to a back table, but Becky sat down, spread her sweater and book over the other two chairs and, when the waitress reached her, said, "I'll have a fruit salad—large. How about you, Pete?"

"Same, I guess. No, wait, a crab sandwich and a Coke," he ordered after looking over the menu. If he were paying, it ought to be something he was sure he liked.

"Crab here is just canned, half the time, but I wouldn't expect *you* to ask anyone," Becky muttered after the waitress had gone.

"What do you mean? What's with you anyhow?" Pete asked. He didn't mind canned crab in sandwiches. It was all right.

"Nothing is wrong with *me.*" Becky leaned over the banister and concentrated on the people below.

So she was mad at him. Becky had these flare-ups, and Pete tried to figure out what he'd done to trigger this one. He wasn't going to get his head bitten off by asking again, though.

Becky continued sulking over the railing until the waitress brought their order. Pete's sandwich had three layers, and a big helping of French fries. It filled the whole plate. He'd never had such a monumental sandwich, and he couldn't resist a grin at Becky.

"See, one-upmanship. Oh, the whole bit. Even this morning. Any normal person would have howled to high heaven and told my mother off. But no, *you* have to act like you're on camera or something." Becky dug angrily into a compote of fresh tropical fruit.

Pete was stunned. His hands felt clammy. He wanted to shout at Becky that he'd thought she was his friend. She was glaring at him like—the guy at the last foster home. "Maybe I'm just not a likable person," he said quietly.

"Oh, come *on,* Pete! Don't look like it's the end of the world. Just listen to me once in a while. You're not the only person in the world with ideas you'd like to talk about, you know. Don't you ever feel low? And I'm sorry about mother—she didn't used to be so paranoiac. Maybe she's going through the change. I don't know—maybe it's just me. I can't seem to get along with any-one—" There were tears in Becky's eyes, and she wiped them angrily with her arm.

Pete wanted to turn and run. He didn't want to be around if she really started crying—especially if it was his fault. And what a laugh about feeling low—maybe he should tell her about his nightmares—

"Can't you see? You can do whatever you want, and I'm stuck, like a prisoner—oh, I don't know, let's eat. I'm sorry."

"No, wait, Becky," Pete stretched his hand across the table. "You want to know how I've been feeling all day? Like I should flip a coin—heads I stick and save the money to get back to Miami and tails I move out right now. Your mom is the only relative I have, and she thinks I'm a thief, and now you—and Uncle Ray calls me 'boy.' Maybe you think I like being anonymous; I can't seem to get along with anyone."

"Hey, that's what I just said."

They looked at each other a long moment, their hands locked tight. Overhead the fan croaked as if it might break down. Down below the crowd had thinned for the siesta, and the streets were nearly quiet. A light breeze from the sea brought a tang of salt and pineapple. Below, the town of Charlotte Amalie spread out in a jumble of colored vines and tiled or corrugated painted aluminum roofs, colorful and mysterious, humid and damp, always seen through the heat haze. And yet here, in this unlikely place, Pete had found someone who felt as he did. His cousin.

"I'd like to be your friend," he said slowly.

Becky nodded, smiling, tentatively at first, but then letting the smile travel up into her eyes. "Me too," she said.

Twenty-Two

The closeness that had come with Becky's revelation that she also felt unlovable soon underwent a strain. One hot afternoon Pete lay on his bed trying to decide what to do next. He'd just talked with Becky, and he was disgusted. It was all very well for Becky to analyze exactly what she thought about herself and everybody else, since *her* parents could hardly kick her out on September fifteenth. And Miami was not the simple alternative she seemed to think, even forgetting about the fare back. If he couldn't even get along with his own flesh-and-blood aunt, what made anyone think life with Barney and Lily would turn out any better? It probably just looked better because he wouldn't be bitten by sand flies in Miami. Maybe they even *had* sand flies in Miami.

The point was that Becky loved heart-to-heart talks. The dumbest single thing he'd ever done in his life was to tell that girl about his nightmares: the last few days she'd been probing to find out just *why* he was interested in fish. The second dumbest thing was coming to see Aunt Lenore and letting himself in for this shoestring-nephew stuff, which amounted to working at least half a day for nothing more than room and board and *still* being considered a charity case. That's what having family did for you.

But when he thought any further, say to the way the clerks at the employment office laughed at him when he asked for a job, it got scary. All anything amounted to was a dead end in every direction.

It would be good to go for a swim, but the moment he set foot on the beach Becky would most likely come galloping up, and he didn't feel up to talking, or to fending her off either. The truth was that he was in the world's lousiest mood, and about the most he *could* do was lie on his mildewy bed. After all, he was entitled to some rest after hoeing sea grape vines all morning.

There was something eerie about the *day* too. There wasn't a breath of air stirring, and the heat came down like an oven. Even the birds were skittish, circling and chattering the way they did in California before a storm. And the sky was a heavy yellow, streaked in red, the color and texture of smog, which was one pain they did not have in the islands. Strange for the middle of the afternoon.

Suddenly Pete sat up and looked out to the sea. The Caribbean is a smooth placid sea, and it was still smooth, but there was a cloudiness and an oiliness he'd never seen before. As he watched, the birds rose high and disappeared. It happened so quickly he could not have said where they flew. Only that when they were gone a profound silence fell over the island. It frightened Pete, and he scrambled out to call the Taylors.

He found Uncle Ray hauling the rowboat up toward the house, pouring sweat and almost purple with the effort. Pete ran down to help him, remembering to slip into zoris before going near the house, a legacy of the refrigerator incident.

"Oh, thanks. Hated to wake you. We knew you still weren't up to par, and God knows when any of us will get more sleep, but I'm glad you're here. Could do with a little help." Together they hauled the boat to cover under the house.

"Is it a hurricane, then?" Pete asked.

"Shouldn't hit until the morning, so we've got time yet. The main thing is to get everything under cover and eat a big dinner tonight. Then we all stick together in the living room and just let her rip—your first?" Uncle Ray grinned, an open friendly smile.

Pete nodded, grinning back, his foul mood forgotten, the heat no longer oppressive but a part of an adventure. He trembled with excitement and could hardly keep his voice steady, as he told Uncle Ray he'd do everything he could to help.

"You're not afraid, then? No, I can see you're not. Good boy. All right, then, let's get the other boat." He followed his uncle back across the hot sand, matching him step for step, alive to the gathering power of sky and sea.

When they entered the kitchen an hour later, Becky was stowing everything—books, lamps, folding furniture —in the low window seats that were built in around the room. Aunt Lenore was setting the table for dinner, and

183

Pete was surprised to find the same eager anticipation that he felt reflected on *her* face.

"Don't forget the veranda furniture, Becky," her father called through the windows—openings without glass or screens so the wind *could* blow on through the house. They would have to duck behind the stone walls for cover from the storm.

"Next on the list," she called back. "And how about the garden tools?" She looked worried.

"We got them."

"I guess we're in for a hurricane, Lenore. Westerly."

"Tempest, dear," she replied, ruffling her husband's hair. "Time for dinner. Better eat all you can, Pete, because I can't guarantee regular meals for the next two or three days."

As Pete smiled back, he thought his aunt was really looking at him for the first time and liking what she saw. She'd said two or three days—seemed like a long time but, of course, it *was* a storm. During dinner a light hot breeze came up, rippling little whitecaps out over the still sea. And then he saw the water begin to churn. He wanted to remember every detail, every change so he could write Barney.

"Why so quiet, Becky?" he asked.

"People *do* get killed in hurricanes, in case you hadn't heard," she said. "Don't frown, Mother. You know it, too. Remember the Pearsons."

"You're going to have to learn that there's no point in worrying over what you can't change, Becky." Her mother's voice was gentle.

Later that night the sea began to move in earnest. Pete was sleeping, as they all were, in the living room of the big house when he was bolted awake by a crack like a rifle shot. Or a car backfiring. Or a tidal wave! He ran to the veranda and found Uncle Ray leaning against the door frame, looking out to the sea. It had risen and the waves rolled in angrily, one after another, like the Pacific during a storm.

"That was just the sea rising, go back to sleep." Then, as Pete still stood looking out, he went on. "I always wanted to go to sea. I suppose most men do. I don't know exactly why. It must be a lonely life, and yet at times like this there's such a pull—well, go back to sleep, boy. You'll need it. You're shivering."

"First time in a month I've been cool," Pete said. The wind had turned cold and it blew steadily in a mounting hum. Pete went back to bed obediently, but sleep seemed out of the question.

The next time, the rain woke him. Woke them all. It was hitting the roof like machine-gun fire, coming down in bursts with a quiet moment in between, just irregular enough to be maddening.

"We're in for it now," Becky groaned.

"At least the cistern will be full." Her father laughed.

"And us drowned along with it."

"*Or* run over by a car the day *after* the hurricane," her mother added cheerfully.

"At least I'll have something to write about after it's over," Pete said.

"That's for sure," Becky agreed.

They fell silent. The night was light enough so they could see that the bay was white with foam and the waves were running in all directions, smashing up against each other and pouring over the reef where Pete and Becky went snorkeling. Pete knew the groupers and parrot fish and even the ancient barracuda who lived at the end of the reef must have headed for the bottom of the sea to wait out the tempest. But the smaller silverfish might not be able to ride out a storm.

Becky shrugged when he asked. "All I know," she said, "is that none of them will be back for a week after a storm. It'll be bright and clear, but not a bird or a fish for days."

"Can't hear you," Pete shouted back.

"Tell you later!"

The noise became incredible as the squall turned into steady driving rain, blown straight across them as they lay huddled low behind the window seats. Conversation was impossible. It seemed to Pete that the ocean was hitting the house.

With dawn he saw that he was right. The wide beach was gone and waves *were* pounding the house, lapping around them! As he watched, one of the rowboats floated down over what had been the beach, was hit by an incoming wave, bounced straight up by the force of the water and smashed as it fell. The general noise was so great that Pete couldn't even hear the boat splinter, though the wind had dropped somewhat.

"Oh, God, did you see *that?*" he yelled to Uncle Ray beside him.

"Yes, I was afraid that rope wasn't tough enough."

"Will we drown?" Pete asked.

"Not a chance!" Becky said cheerfully. She had apparently gotten over her earlier fright. "Mom, let's have some breakfast."

Aunt Lenore calmly sat under the table making peanut butter sandwiches.

186

"Don't dally over them. And eat an orange, but quickly." She looked as if she hadn't slept, but her smile was warm. "And Ray, don't get any ideas about checking anything," she warned as her husband stood up and stretched.

"No, Ma'am. Our tenderfoot's doing pretty well, don't you think?"

"It's in the blood," she said, reaching over and ruffling Pete's hair.

Becky wound her watch. It was 8:30 A.M.

Before they finished their sandwiches, the wind was on them again, with a vengeance. If the wind had blown and the water whipped before, it tore them now. The rain fell as if the sky were emptying.

All that day and the next night the storm lashed and the sea drove against the house until it seemed impossible that they could survive, impossible that the noises— the roar of water, the creaking, groaning house, the palms bent until their fronds slapped water, the driving wind— would ever stop. Pete was too tired finally to move, to worry. Whatever came, came. Hell must be like this, he thought. He didn't even try to watch anymore. Neither did Becky or her father, who kept an arm around her as he had around Pete earlier. Only Aunt Lenore peered out at the storm until the night closed in again. Then she sighed, turned around, and took Pete's hand, rubbing it between her own.

"Just smell the sea air," she shouted during a lull.

"I can't smell anything else," Becky shouted back, and they all laughed, high-pitched and nervous, like horses whinnying.

Sometime during that night Pete fell asleep, his hand

still gripping Aunt Lenore's. Her ring rubbed annoyingly, but he hated to let go.

By the next morning, the wind had slackened. This time Pete did not ask if the storm was over. He was exhausted. He felt as if he had lived through a nightmare and been thrown up on the beach. He ate the cold canned spaghetti Uncle Ray handed him and lay down again. Becky did not wake up for breakfast. Uncle Ray and Aunt Lenore moved warily, looking out on the destruction.

"Not too bad, everything considered," Uncle Ray said.

"It's this house. We would have been safe even if we'd washed out to sea."

"Like Wynken, Blynken, and Nod?" Uncle Ray laughed and kissed her gently. "Well, we've made it again, Pete."

"I guess." Pete still had to shout over the wind.

By midday it was all over. The four of them stood on the veranda and looked over the beach. The trees were stripped bare, but the beach was heaped with coral, seaweed, and fish, even a few octopuses. There was no trace of the broken rowboat. Absence of noise was as overwhelming as the din of the hurricane had been. Pete looked over at Becky, who was breathing deeply and doing knee bends.

"Practicing being alive," she said.

"Well, Lenore, cleanup time again?" Uncle Ray said, taking her hand. And then turning to Pete, "There'll certainly be enough gardening for a while."

"At least it's been watered." If there was such a thing as a kind sense of humor, Pete decided Uncle Ray had one.

"And you've been initiated, Pete. When you go back to the mainland, you can tell your friends you're an islander now." Aunt Lenore laughed.

"And when you come back next summer, we'll arrange a repeat performance," Uncle Ray added, slapping him on the back.

"Yes, yes, I will," Pete said and knew he'd made his decision.

Twenty-Three

Two days after the hurricane Pete went into town, slipping off before Becky could decide to go along or before anyone could ask why he was going.

It was early afternoon when he returned, and he hoped to go on down to the beach unnoticed while the rest were napping. The beach was almost clean again, the debris raked into huge piles that they would burn. He was aching for a swim.

Aunt Lenore sat on the veranda drinking iced tea and staring out to sea.

"I've been waiting for you," she said.

"I left a note."

"I know. Sit down. Care for a Coke?"

He nodded. He could hear Aunt Lenore slapping across the kitchen in her zoris, opening the refrigerator door and shaking out ice cubes. He still tensed when he heard the squeak of that door, sensing again the shock so acutely it left his nerve endings raw. In addition, his aunt's behavior indicated a heart-to-heart talk. But, with his news, he ought to be able to head *that* off.

"Pete, we've had a series of nieces and nephews show up here, and I'm sorry it took a tempest for me to separate you from the pack; but you can always tell an islander by the way he reacts to his first hurricane. Most people panic but, once in a great while, somebody comes along who appreciates the fireworks. And can lend a hand —we were grateful."

"Thanks." Pete concentrated on rolling a piece of ice around in his mouth. Finally he looked up and into his aunt's eyes.

"Maybe you'd better tell me a little more about yourself," she said quietly.

"My plans, you mean?"

"Those too—but what brought you here this summer, for starters? Uncle Ray and I haven't asked questions— two reasons—we wanted to give you a chance to settle first—and we haven't been sure we wanted to get involved. Now we are."

Pete thought desperately. The thing to do was tell her his plans—elaborately—and then she'd forget about why he was here.

"We haven't even phoned your foster parents," she said.

"I ran away," Pete whispered, trapped.

"I kind of figured that. Want to tell me why?"

"They were going to adopt me, and I heard them saying what a pain in the neck I was—" And once started Pete told her about meeting Barney, their trip and life in the carnival together, the trailer court in Florida, and his first day in the Virgin Islands. She listened intently and, when he had finished, shook her head.

"It's quite a bit of mileage to get out of one summer, Pete, I'll say that for it. And I can't fault you for leaving that home. Shows guts. So, now what do you have in mind?"

"That's what I was doing in town, phoning Lily to tell her I'll be back in Florida in time for school— September fifteenth."

"Well, you've a standing invitation to come back here every summer until you or I die—and that's an invitation I've never given another relative. But that won't help you get back into school. How would it be—would you like me to phone the welfare people, tell them you're here and that I'll sign whatever release they need—what do they call it—a responsible relative—just so they know you're all right and can clear their files. Or is that meddling?" she asked with a grin.

"Then I won't be a fugitive."

"Disappoint you?"

"Not really. I've been afraid Lily might get into trouble." Pete didn't add he'd also been worried that they might extradite him to California when he tried to start school. He looked out on the play of sun and shadows over the bay, wanting a swim, wondering how long this was going on. Talking about himself made him uneasy. Still, it *was* a break that Aunt Lenore was going to sign for him.

"The one thing that puzzles me is how you're going to get your schooling if this Lily keeps moving around so much."

"She says she'll stay put until we get through." Pete

shrugged. He was worried about the moving too. "I just feel comfortable with them," he said finally. "I know that maybe Lily can't stay put—still—"

It was her turn to nod. "Well, it's probably the best for right now. I can't make this a promise, but we'll see if we can't be of a little help when you get to college. I hope you keep on with the marine biology." This last was shyly said, as if she felt she were overstepping.

"Why?" Pete asked, because it was a question he'd been asking himself.

"Because I think you like the sea, have a feeling for it—"

"You do, too, like the sea?" It was Pete's turn to be hesitant. He remembered his aunt during the hurricane. He remembered her sitting up all night watching, her eyes darting about so she wouldn't miss a thing.

"I should have gone to sea," she said flatly.

Pete believed her. He could see that it would have suited her. There didn't seem to be anything to say. Now it was too late anyhow. He didn't remember ever hearing of women going to sea. He thought of asking why she didn't go sailing, but he knew that would not be the same and so he didn't say that either. He also remembered Uncle Ray saying he should have gone to sea. Strange. He sat tracing the hibiscus pattern in the chair cushion with his index finger, wondering what to *do*.

"Can't be helped. You run on and get a swim now. I may join you in a few minutes myself." She stood up. "Oh, Pete, would fifty dollars settle our gardening bill?"

Pete had started for the door, but he turned and faced his aunt. "You don't have to pay me."

She laughed. "I always meant to, you know."

193

"Did Becky tell you I need forty bucks more for plane fare?"

"She said you planned to ask neighbors for gardening jobs this next week. We'd rather take you on the grand tour of the island. And, besides, you've earned this."

"Thanks. Thanks a lot." Pete held out his hand, and his aunt took it and briefly held it to her cheek.

"Now scoot," she said.

The next week was given over to taking Pete about the island of St. Thomas. For the first time he heard a steel band, went sailing and snorkeling off the side of a boat, toured the elegant shops of Charlotte Amalie, which seemed more like museums than stores filled with goods anyone could actually own. One day they spent an hour each on seven popular beaches. Another day they lunched in the mountains, surrounded by tropical birds and orchids. Pete had never *been* entertained before and, as the week ended, he began to have the melancholy feeling that the very best time in his life was ending.

It was in this mood that he started out with Becky for the ruins of an old sugar plantation three miles from their house. They walked single file along a narrow footpath that cut across a jungle of sea grape and oleander, then through a mango grove, and finally broke out into a green meadow. Here and there a shack made of flattened tin cans or a small unpainted cabin with a corrugated tin roof stood along the path. There seemed to Pete to be dozens of people lounging about each house. More voices and laughter came from inside the cabins. It was the laughter that Pete wanted to fix in his mind and that made him feel particularly sad. There seemed to be so much more laughter on this island than anywhere else he'd been.

If he asked Aunt Lenore, she might let him stay. Maybe he could live here with his *own* family. For a moment it was a tempting idea. He liked them all now, and they liked him. He wouldn't have to leave St. Thomas at all.

But the truth, Pete reluctantly acknowledged, was that he'd rather live with Barney and Lily. Perhaps rather wasn't quite the word—it wasn't like busting in on a family. They were odd men out in a way, like him, and that made it comfortable. He had a place there, and he didn't feel like a guest—or a shoestring relative. Thanks to Barney he also had a job and could pay his way.

Besides, Aunt Lenore had specified summer vacations —period. Summers were a time for visiting relatives. It wasn't as if he'd never see St. Thomas again. He didn't have to memorize every leaf on the island. He'd be *back* in nine months, after all.

"We're almost there," Becky called back without breaking her loping walk. It was the first time she'd spoken since they left the house.

Pete was used to Becky's long silences. He found it companionable to be with a girl who wasn't always talking. She made up for it when she did.

"There it is. You can see the old plantation house, and way over to the left is what's left of the mill itself, A couple of hundred people lived here once," Becky added dreamily. Aunt Lenore *had said* it was one of Becky's make-believe places.

Pete looked out over what appeared to be the ruins of a small town. Stone foundations and walls cropped up like mushrooms from the lush green undergrowth. Here .and there a complete room, lacking only the roof, re-

195

mained. He counted fourteen separate buildings and, as he did he felt a chill, as if he were trespassing or somehow invading the privacy of the dead man who had once stood on this same hill, overseeing his plantation.

Only a few of the buildings were being used but the soft laughter was reminder enough of the bustle that had once made this valley a producing sugar plantation. It wasn't hard to see why this was a special place for a solitary girl like Becky. What better place to dream than an abandoned town? But he wondered if she brought him today because she was *already* lonely because he'd been so wrapped up in his plans for leaving. Pete sighed. He struggled to remember what it was Becky had just said.

"Some still do," Pete answered, indicating portions of the decaying plantation house walls that had corrugated iron sheets thrown between them to act as makeshift roofs. A strange stillness lay over this old plantation, a hush, as though the dead still ruled here.

"What happened? Why did they go?" Pete whispered.

"My dad says sugar prices fell because they started growing beets for sugar on the mainland. Mom says they had a diphtheria epidemic, so you can take your choice." Becky smiled for the first time. "Let's have our lunch over by the mill. At least there's a little privacy there." She indicated an old stone mill with its brown cone rising out of the pervading greenery. It stood on a small knoll.

"Smells like vanilla," Pete said.

"Those are the vanilla orchids—when it's still like this you can smell them for miles, seems like. Race you to the mill!"

Becky took off like a deer, but Pete soon found that stone foundations and loose stones were everywhere, covered by grass and vines so they were great booby traps. He made his way slowly and wonderingly across the old mansion, trying to guess what rooms and what outbuildings each pile of gray stones indicated.

When he reached Becky, she was leaning disconsolately against the mill, looking out over the trees to the ocean. She looked as if she had been crying.

"Pete, are you really going? Really? This has been the best week I've ever had."

"Me too," he said sadly. "But I'll be back next year."

"Might as well be next century. I don't know what I'll do without you," Becky said, and the tears were ready to spill again.

"No one's ever said that to me before."

"I'm the first cousin you've ever had, too."

"And the best."

As if they were embarrassed by the sudden confidences and afraid to go further into their feelings, both fell silent. They sat together, looking out over the abandoned sugarcane. fields, to the sea, so tranquil that it reflected the sky. It was midday and the heat rose in damp waves, pleasant enough if one sat quietly and let the island have its way. An occasional bird and the sound of soft laughter from the shacks broke the silence, and over them the smallest breeze carried the smell of the vanilla orchid and the faint sense of salt from the sea.

"Maybe," Pete said drowsily. "Maybe you can come to Florida and visit me—Lily loves company." Pete smiled then, partly because of the way Becky's face lit up and also because this was the first time in his life he had ever invited anyone to *his* home.

197